NO MORE DARKNESS

STACEY WILK

TITLE

Copyright © 2019 by Stacey Wilk

Cover design copyright © 2023 by Jen Talty

ISBN: (ebook edition) 978-0-9896128-6-9

ISBN: (paperback edition) 978-0-9896128-7-6

Printed in the USA

To Josh and Sam
You are my true joy.

CHAPTER ONE

Aria needed to be in Cape May by tonight. The snow made it impossible to see out the windshield. She turned up her windshield wipers, but that did little to help. The winter storm had come up from the south at break neck speed and ruined her plans because she and every other car on the Garden State Parkway moved along at a crawl.

She turned up the defroster then fished inside her purse for some gum. Her fingers brushed across thick board paper and pulled out the invitation instead. The style was Letterpress and pricey. She had forgotten she put the invitation in her purse at the last second. She wasn't even sure why she did it except the couple was full of love and hope for their future. More so than other clients she had worked with recently. Very much the way she and Hawk had been a long time ago.

The vehicle in front of her picked up speed.

"Finally." She gave the car some gas. Maybe she'd get to the hotel with time to spare.

The same car slammed on the brakes. She did too. Her back tires skidded on the wet and icy pavement. She pressed the brake pedal further to the floor, but the car didn't respond. She yanked the wheel and the wedding favors in the back clanked together like chimes blowing in the wind. She winced. Those favors could not break. She missed the front car by inches and came to stop. She gulped in air to slow her heart. The favors were safe.

A bang and jolt sent her forward, but the seatbelt jerked her back. Her head bounced against the seat's headrest. "What the hell?" She turned in her seat to see who had hit her.

"Oh, no, no, no." She shoved out of the car and slipped in the snow. Her arms air planed, but she gripped the back door handle before she landed on her butt.

This wasn't happening. "Why weren't you paying attention?" She yelled to the driver who hit her with his big Lexus SUV.

His car had no damage, but her rear wheel frame was crushed against the tire. The tire was flatter than her boobs. The hatch that hadn't worked right in years had flown open. Some of the wedding favors spilled out of the back of her car and all over the road. The rose-colored, stemless wine glasses imprinted with the bride and groom's names were nothing more than pink glitter in the snow. She was ruined. She'd be known as the worst wedding planner ever.

The man from the Lexus came over. "I'm so sorry. Are you all right? When you skidded you got right in front of me. I couldn't stop in time with the wet roads."

"What am I supposed to do with this mess?"

Other cars honked as they went past. Of course, the

traffic moved along at a better speed now. Just her luck. A woman went by and gave her the finger.

"Are you kidding me about now?" She yelled to the retreating taillights of the bitch in the car.

"I already called the police for help. My insurance will take care of everything," the Lexus man said.

"Is your insurance company going to take care of the broken wedding favors I need in three days?" She would have to reimburse the bride for the ones that broke. It might be the only way to save face.

This wedding was supposed to take her business to the next level. Celine Wood was the picture-perfect bride. She was tall, beautiful, smart, and came from a prominent family who liked to spend money on their children. Most of Celine's bridesmaids were potential clients as well as the two hundred and fifty guests expected to attend this wedding.

"Can I help you clean this up?" The Lexus man's smile faltered on his blotchy red face.

She should give the guy a break. He was trying to be nice. "What's your name?"

"Billy."

"Billy, I'm Aria. I don't have a broom, and the snow is doing a pretty good job of covering the glass. I think I'm pretty much screwed, but thanks."

Red and blue lights turned the falling white powder into a purple snow cone. A state trooper's vehicle came up the center lane and parked sideways to direct traffic to the right. The trooper unfolded himself from the front seat. He pulled his cap down low on his head and marched over.

"Would you two please get back in your cars?"

"Officer, I need to get to Cape May. This was an accident. Can we just exchange information and get on with it?"

"Ma'am, it's dangerous out here. Even on the side of the road, with this storm, you're at risk. Staying in your vehicles at this point would be best."

She reached into her glove compartment and pulled out the necessary paperwork. "I'm Aria Scirocco, and this is Billy. Here's my info. Billy, go get your stuff and give it to the police officer." She waved him away.

"Of course. I'll be right back."

"You're going to need a tow. I'll call for one," the trooper said.

"I can't let you tow it with my stuff in the back." She had to make the cop understand the magnitude of her situation.

"You can take your belongings with you." The trooper's voice carried the distinct sound of patience lost.

"Can you help me pull the fender away from the tire? I have a spare." She gripped the bent metal and tugged, but it wouldn't budge.

"Ma'am, that isn't going to work." He put a gentle hand on her shoulder.

"I see that." She did not want to accept defeat, but the stern look on the trooper's face told her she might have to start.

"The car can't stay here. You might be able to push it to the shoulder, but you'll need a towing company. Call a friend to come and help you. I'll send for the tow truck." He handed her back her license and registration.

"But, Officer, I need my car." She wouldn't call anyone to come out in this storm, and she could not go with her car to wherever it would be towed because she had to get to the hotel.

Billy ran up and offered over his identification. He said to her, "I really am sorry about your car."

"Thanks, me too. Can we get this over with, please?"

"Officer, do you need some help?" A male voice drifted across the wind and landed with the snowflakes on the broken wedding favors.

"What are you doing here?" she said through clenched teeth. It wasn't possible, but she guessed it was because there he stood.

"Sir, is this your wife? Please tell me it's your wife." The cop rolled his eyes.

"She was once." Hawk Egan smile's spread wide and showed all his perfect teeth. His hair hung low and curled at his collar, just the way she liked it. His beard dusted his face. He hadn't shaved today, and she hated that she knew that. His flannel shirt hung untucked over faded jeans that bunched at untied boots. He didn't wear a coat as if he couldn't care less about the weather, and knowing him, that was probably the case.

"You didn't answer my question. What are you doing here?"

"Of all the gin joints…" He smirked.

"Please stop quoting Humphrey Bogart and answer my question." He should not have the power to boil her blood after all this time, but he did.

"Could you two take yourselves off the road? Ma'am, a tow truck is on the way. I suggest you take your things out of your car and grab a ride from him." The trooper hitched his thumb toward Hawk.

The tow truck arrived. The driver waddled to the back of his truck and dropped the flatbed.

"Where are you headed? I'll give you a ride," Hawk said.

The snow had snuck inside her coat and made her cold to the bone. She'd lost the feeling in her toes because her boots were better for fashion than function. She glanced at the tow truck with its flashing yellow lights on the roof and back at Hawk. If she went with the tow truck, how would she get back to the Cape?

Hawk had always known what she needed before he'd started drinking. His appearance at her time of crisis should surprise her more than it did.

She turned to Hawk. "Please be honest and tell me how you knew I was here."

A darkness passed over his light-brown eyes. "I could tell you I was out for a drive. You'd believe I had no destination."

They had fought about that very thing more than once. "Is that what you're telling me?"

"Does it matter? I'm here. I'll give you a ride."

"Lady, go with your husband," the officer said.

"Ex-husband."

"Whatever. The report will be ready in ten business days. Now, get off the road."

"You heard the man. That guy or me?" Hawk pointed to the tow truck driver.

Both choices sat in her stomach like broken glass. She had a job to do. Her bride depended on her. Grabbing a ride from Hawk had nothing to do with him.

Nothing. At. All.

CHAPTER TWO

Hawk put the last of Aria's boxes in the back of his truck and closed the bed cover. The tow truck took her car to the auto-body shop right off the exit. He promised to drive her to the Hotel Horseman on the island, and he would do it. Then he'd get right back in his truck and on his way to his real destination.

He hitched his leg inside the cab and closed the door shutting out the cold and the snow. He should've worn his coat out there. "Are you cold?" He didn't wait for her to answer and turned up the heat.

"Better now. Thank you for the ride." She wrung her hands in her lap.

He resisted the urge to cover her hands with his own and pulled back onto the Parkway. "You're welcome."

Her red hair was longer than the last time he saw her. The ends had curled down her back in a way that made his fingers want to touch it. The inside of the cab filled with her earthy perfume. She still smelled great. He shifted in his seat. She kept her gaze out the window. He wished she'd look his way.

They drove over the draw bridge and into the small sea side town. The streets narrowed and the cottages lined up alongside each other with very little space between them. The snow fell through the yellow glow of the lantern-style street lights making the sleepy island town warm and inviting.

This detour messed with his arrival at the hotel in Virginia, but when he heard the accident over the scanner, he had to see if she was okay. She wouldn't accept his appearance any other way. She had rebuffed all his other attempts before now.

"Another wedding?" He needed to fill the space with something other than his thoughts.

"What's that?" She turned from the window.

"All those wine glasses I just put in the back of my truck, I assume you're planning another wedding." He didn't know what to say to her. He'd never been great at small talk. That had been one of her complaints about him while they were married.

"This is the biggest wedding I've ever done. It could mean a lot more business for me." A smile tugged at her lips.

He missed seeing her smile at him. "Good luck then."

"Thanks." She flipped her hair off her shoulder. Something glittered on her hand.

His breath sputtered like an old engine. "Did you get engaged?"

She looked at the huge rock on her finger. "I was going to tell you."

"When?" The one word came out as a growl. He

gripped the steering wheel until his knuckles turned white. He believed he'd get another shot with her. He thought he had more time.

"I haven't had a chance. It's not like we see each other anywhere."

"Your crowd doesn't run with mine, right?"

"Hawk, don't start this again."

He wanted to start it, and he wanted to finish it too, but the Hotel Horseman rose up at the end of the road with its six floors and white columns. The large windows welcomed guests with their warm light and view of the lobby. He pulled into the circular driveway by the front door. "I'll help you unload."

The salty smell of the ocean hung in the air along with the storm clouds. The snow continued to cover every flat surface. The storm wasn't letting up. The wind shoved him around, but he kept his head down and grabbed boxes.

Aria dove in and took as many boxes as he did. She wasn't going to allow him to handle this for her. He didn't want to take over. He only wanted to help. "I can take your suitcase." He lifted it out of the back.

"That's not necessary. I've got it from here. Thanks."

"Where do all those boxes have to go?" They had left the boxes right inside the double doors.

"The ballroom, but I can handle it."

He should just walk away. She made it clear how she felt the day she left him. Still, he couldn't stop himself when it came to her. He wanted to help her and make her life easier. That's all he ever wanted. "I'll just carry them to the ballroom, then I'll go."

He didn't wait for her to argue. He carried the boxes

through the lobby and into the ballroom. She was fast on his heels with a box in her hands for every two he carried.

"I guess that's it. Thank you for the help." She rummaged around in her big tote bag. "Here. For your troubles." She waved wrinkled money in her fist.

"Oh, hell no. I'm not taking your money." He shoved his hands in his pockets.

"Why not?"

"Because we were married." And because he would never take money from her for anything. She stared at him with her creased forehead as if she couldn't understand him. That might have been their problem all along.

"I took your money when we were married. Here."

He gripped her wrist. Her soft skin sent a warm sensation up his arm and right to his chest. The feel of her always had him wanting to touch her more. "That was different. We shared. Now you're just insulting me. Give your money to your fiancé. I don't need it."

Her mouth opened and closed. "I understand you're upset, but you had to know this would happen someday. You've been with other women since me."

He had gone to bed with other women since their divorce two years ago, but there had never been another woman who could grab his heart the way Aria did. "You got that right."

He turned on his heel knowing his remark would hurt her. Finding out she was ready to remarry cut him. He stopped moving, but kept his back to her. "I'm sorry, Aria. I shouldn't have said that."

"Go, Hawk. Whatever aimless place you were driving to, just go. I have a job to do."

The lights flickered and went out. Some people called out from the other rooms. The ballroom was black as ink. He could not see his hand in front of his face.

"Hawk?" Her voice wobbled. She must still hate the dark.

"I'm right here. Don't move. The generator will kick on in a second." He took a step toward her heavy breathing and grabbed her arm. She took his hand and laced her cold fingers through his. He gave her hand a squeeze so she'd know he wouldn't let anything happen to her. That was their old signal.

"I'm sorry I told you to go away."

"Don't sweat it. We were both angry. The generator should've kicked in by now. Come on, let's go see what's going on."

Still holding her hand, he followed the sounds of guests asking questions and the glow from the fireplaces. The lobby was drafty and cloaked in shadows. Some people had turned on the flashlight app on their phones.

"I'll go ask at the desk. Stay here."

She nodded.

A couple was at the front desk bending the ear of the hotel employee. "But when will the lights come back on?" the guy with a dark ski jacket said.

"I'm not entirely sure. We're working on it," the man behind the front desk with the name tag reading Henry, hung up the phone.

"Michael, I can't stay here in these conditions," Ski Jacket said to his partner.

"Ethan, we can't go anywhere. Please deal with it."

"Did you call the electrician?" he said over Michael and Ethan.

"We did, sir. But he can't get here. The police department called to say the bridge is stuck in the up position."

"Did you say stuck?" Hawk said.

"Yes, sir. No one is getting on or off the island tonight."

CHAPTER THREE

She was doomed. How could she pull off a wedding without power? Half the favors were broken with no way of replacing them, and no one could get to the hotel from the main land. The centerpieces weren't here yet, the photographer, the band, and most importantly the groom and his groomsmen. Aria could only hope that her bride listened to her and came this morning before the weather hit. The ladies were going to get pampered before the big event. She hadn't had a chance to check yet.

Her purse and suitcase were in the ballroom. She pushed out a long breath. Her phone was in her purse. She wasn't going back in the dark alone. It was stupid to be afraid of the dark at her age, but she was. Only Hawk had never made fun of her for it. He was sweet like that. It was his other habits that were the problem.

He sauntered back to her with his crooked smile. His casual, rugged style still made her knees weak. She had to remind herself marrying the bad boy was a mistake.

She turned her engagement ring on her finger. A man like Patrick was the kind of man to build a life with. Patrick worked in the financial district in Manhattan. He was stable, reliable, responsible. He planned everything just like she did. He gave her advice on how to run her business, even though he wasn't a fan of the wedding industry. Her mind told her he was perfect on paper, and that should be enough, but her heart tried to tell her something else.

"The hotel is booked solid." Hawk shoved his hands in his jeans pockets.

"I'm not following."

"I can't get off the island and the hotel is booked up. No rooms available."

"There must be a bed and breakfast with rooms to rent. It's January at the shore." She pushed away from the arm of the sofa. He could not stay in this hotel with her.

"Aria, the storm is getting worse. I'm not going out tonight. In the morning, I'll get back on the road. Can I camp out in your room?"

"Oh, no, Hawk Egan. That is not happening. You can't sleep with me."

He leaned in, and she could smell his oaky scent. "I would like nothing more than to sleep with you, but I'll settle for a spot on the floor. I'll even keep my clothes on unless you tell me otherwise."

She groaned. "You are impossible. I'm engaged to someone else." Someone who was expecting her to check-in when she got to the hotel. If she didn't, he'd call and text until she did. He cared about her, which was nice, but she wondered if he cared too much.

"You were mine first."

"I'm not a toy to fight over."

"That you are not, but I will gladly take my chances in a fight against your fiancé."

Hawk had been in a lot of fights over the years, and she didn't like it because it reminded her too much of her father. She always held her breath when Hawk's anger surfaced. He never hit her. She was never worried about that. She worried someone else would kill him one day.

"You will do no such thing. Stay away from Patrick."

"Okay, okay, no fighting." He held his hands up in surrender. Jest twinkled in his eyes.

She fought the urge to laugh. It would just encourage him. "I need to get to my bags in the ballroom. Would you walk with me?"

He offered his arm and she took it. He was a man of few words. Sometimes that was great and others not so much, but tonight she appreciated his quiet resoluteness.

"You never told me how you knew I was on the Parkway." They passed through a room decorated in dark brown. The fireplace burned here too.

"If I tell you, will you let me stay in your room?"

She was actually thinking that very thing. She gave his muscular arm a squeeze. "Fine, but on the floor with all your clothes on."

"Fair enough. I heard the call on the scanner. I recognized your license plate number."

It was so simple, she should have thought of it. "You did that on purpose."

Inside the dark ballroom, he turned on the light from his phone. "What's that?"

"Made me think you were just out in a snowstorm for no good reason." She slung her tote on her shoulder.

"You thought that all by yourself, sweetheart. You made your mind up about me a long time ago, and there has been nothing that has changed it."

"Can we call a truce tonight?" It was late and her neck hurt from the accident. She could use a hot bath and a glass of wine, not a fight with him. He'd be gone in the morning. They could go back to their separate corners.

"So, I'm right then? You still believe the worst about me." He didn't back down.

"What's different? Why now? You've made promises before you couldn't keep. Why should I believe you?" The hurt still burned a hole in her heart. She had loved him like no one else, not even Patrick, and he had let her down more than once.

"You know what? You shouldn't. I'm still the same asshole you divorced. Haven't learned a thing. Thanks for the room, but I think I'll sleep in my truck. Turn on your flashlight app. You're on your own." He waited for her to find her phone then he extinguished his light.

"Good night, Aria." He turned to go.

She couldn't let him sleep in his truck. He'd freeze to death. The storm still hollered outside. Even if he could find a B&B with a room, he shouldn't be driving. He was mad and probably not focused. She didn't need his accident on her conscience if something happened.

"Hawk, wait." She swallowed the knot in her throat.

He stopped and faced her. "What?"

"I'm sorry I said what I did. I guess if we could get along, we wouldn't be divorced. Please stay with me tonight. I don't want you driving or sleeping outside in this weather." She still loved him deep down. He would always have a piece of her heart.

He walked over and took the tote off her shoulder. He handled the suitcase with precision and swaggered out of the ballroom without another word. She hurried after him with her light.

She just had to get to the morning. He'd be on the road again, and she could go back to planning the wedding of her career if the power came back on and the bridge was operational.

She had a better life without him. That's what she told herself every day.

One time, she might actually believe it.

Hawk grabbed the blankets and extra pillows out of the closet. The king size bed took up most of the room, and the floor sloped toward the windows. If he didn't roll in his sleep, he might be okay. He could handle one night with Aria. He had spent plenty of nights in the same room with her angry back to him. Why should tonight be any different?

Because he wanted her to believe he could change. He had changed. When she left him after Wyatt died, it was the kick in the ass he needed to pull his act together. He had planned to show her how much, but every time he thought he was ready, he stalled.

He knocked on the bathroom door. "Are you hungry?" His stomach growled as if the question was directed at it.

She opened the door a couple of inches. The flickering light of candle flames bathed her in gold light. The white hotel robe hung to the floor on her. She had tied up her hair, revealing her long, creamy neck. His lips missed the taste of her skin. He tried to slow his breath and not think about what she didn't have on under the robe.

"Did the power come back on?" She dragged his thoughts back to the present.

"Not yet. I thought I'd go down to the lobby. Maybe they'll let me poke around in the kitchen."

She laughed, and his chest puffed up. "You will probably find a way to be running the kitchen. Anything you can scrounge up would be great. I'm starving."

"Are you going to be okay while I'm gone?"

"I'll be fine. Thank you for never throwing that in my face."

He leaned against the doorjamb to get closer to her. His fingers itched to touch her face. He shoved them in his pockets. "Not my style. Now, if you were Phoenix or even Wyatt, I would definitely have poked fun at that, but never you."

She opened the door a few more inches. "How are you holding up without Wyatt?"

"Fine. I'll be back soon." He took the hotel room key and his phone out into the hallway.

He wasn't ready to talk about Wyatt with her. He didn't talk about him much at all. Not even when Phoenix brought him up. He missed his older brother every day, and the guilt threatened to choke him most of the time. But he learned to keep putting one foot in front of the other. His work with the grief organization helped.

He wouldn't be getting to the retreat any time soon with the storm. They would have to start without him. He sent a quick text to Phoenix and told him about the storm. He left out the part about Aria.

He went in search of the kitchen and some food. He might only have tonight to start to show her he was different. Mostly different. He'd never be the kind of talker she wanted, but maybe he could be the man she needed.

More than whoever the fuck Patrick was.

CHAPTER FOUR

Aria's stomach growled, reminding her she hadn't eaten since the morning. She hurried out of the robe before Hawk came back. She drew on a pair of sweats and reached for her favorite sweatshirt, but stopped. The fire department logo in the corner against the faded navy fleece stared at her. The shirt had been Hawk's. She could never get rid of it or give it back to him. When he moved out, it had been in her hamper because she wore it all the time, loving the feel of it against her skin and his scent woven in the fabric. She kept it as a reminder of the good times together. Her engagement ring caught the flicker of the candlelight. She put the sweatshirt under her other clothes and grabbed her phone.

Patrick had left three voice mail messages like she suspected. His constant hovering closed up her airway. Hawk always gave her space to roam. She had misunderstood that gesture as not caring about her, or being too wrapped up in his own stuff to notice her. She may have been wrong about that.

She risked a quick call even though her battery was low. It was time. This call should have happened much sooner but she had avoided it. The storm changed all that.

The phone rang and rang. Voice mail answered. "You've reached Patrick Phillips. I'm with a client. Please leave a message."

She waited for the beep. "It's me. Call me in the morning. I need to talk to you." She ended the call and shot a quick text to her bride.

Hi. Have you arrived at the hotel?

Hi! My ladies and I are here. Power?

Well, Celine and her bridesmaids on the premises was one less thing to worry about. She responded with, *IDK.*

I'm concerned about the generators.

Don't be. I'll see what I can do.

Aria had no idea what she could do about the loss of power or the bridge or the broken favors she neglected to mention. She didn't know what she was going to do about her ex-husband sleeping on the floor of her hotel room either.

The rattling of the old-fashioned key in the door interrupted her thoughts. This hotel honored its history by giving guests an authentic, gold key instead of a swipe card. The homage to an older, simpler time is what made the bride choose the location.

A smile tugged at her lips as Hawk came through the door holding a tray with food and wine on it. The candle light and the satisfied smirk on his face only managed to make him more handsome.

"I scored." He shut the door and engaged the chain.

"How did you manage that?" She cleared space on the desk for the tray filled with grapes, cheese, crackers, pretzels, two slices of chocolate cake, and a bottle of wine.

"I flexed my pec muscles." He winked.

"Stop it. You did not." She popped a grape in her mouth and moaned. "Maybe it's because I'm so hungry, but this is so sweet."

He poured the wine into a glass and handed it to her. Their fingers grazed as she took the glass. The shock of his touch almost made her drop the wine.

"Okay, I didn't flex. I told her my wife was starving and when she got hungry, she has been known to be dangerous. I pleaded for my life."

The laughter fizzled on her tongue and tickled her nose. He could always make her laugh. "You charmed a pretty lady, didn't you?"

"I've been known to be charming from time to time." He sliced the wedge of brie cheese.

"You can be very charming when you want to be." She glanced at him over the rim of her glass.

"Are you flirting with me?" He handed her a small plate with cheese and crackers. The humor was back in his eyes.

"You would think that." She sat on the bed and curled her feet under her, needing to cool down the space between them.

"So, you weren't?" He opened the complimentary water bottle on the side table.

"I was not. I don't flirt with strange men."

"You just share a room with them?" He raised an eyebrow.

"I walked right into that. Change of subject, why aren't you having any of the wine with me?"

He dropped into the desk chair. "I don't drink anymore. I've been sober for two years, six months, and twenty-nine days." He raised his water in salute.

The day she left him. "That's great. I'm glad." Her father had never been able to stop drinking. It was his alcoholism that killed him. Now, Hawk would a have a chance at a good life. That's all she wanted for him.

"Tell me about your fiancé." He took a bite of the chocolate cake. The crumbs tumbled over his lap and onto the floor.

She resisted the urge to tell him to grab a napkin. "Why do you want to know about him?"

"I want to know who my competition is."

"Hawk, there is no competition. You and I are through." Still, the idea that he even wanted a chance sent a warm shiver over her skin. He heart crossed out the practical list her mind created for marrying Patrick. Patrick rarely made her shiver with anticipation.

"I'm going to brush my teeth. It's been a long day." He pushed out of the chair.

She didn't want him to run off just yet. They were having a good moment, and she wanted it to keep going. "Aren't you going to eat more? You barely touched the food."

"I'm not that hungry. Try the cake. It's your favorite. I wasn't lying about how you get when you don't eat.

Finish your snack." He winked again and went into the bathroom, closing the door.

And shutting her out. Some things never changed. Her heart ached at the thought of the good times they had together. It had been easier to remember the bad times. If she remembered how much it hurt when he didn't show up when he said he would, or the fighting, or the drinking, then she wouldn't want to love him like she did. Moving on allowed her to meet Patrick and get a second chance at happiness.

She had been happy with Hawk; with Patrick it had been about the plans and the schedule. Patrick liked to do what he liked to do, and if she wouldn't go along, he'd pout. With Patrick, happiness came in a different color and size.

Hawk would do anything with her, even yoga, as long as they did it together. She hadn't thought about that in some time.

She wondered if Hawk still slept in his boxer briefs like he used to, or if the touch of his skin against hers could ignite a flame that never burned out.

Sex was an area she struggled with since Hawk left. Patrick didn't seem to notice the lack of passion or the rote moves he performed. She often needed to conjure Hawk's face in order to moan at all the right times, and worse, to reach a climax. Not every relationship would be filled with hot sex. She had passion with Hawk. She must've used up her quota.

Hawk came back into the room wearing shorts and a t-shirt. Disappointment tapped her on the shoulder that he wasn't bare chested. She brushed the feeling away.

He dumped his duffle in the corner. "Do you need the bathroom? I want to put out the candles."

"We can't sleep with them burning?"

"Not safe." He unzipped his bag and handed her a flashlight. "Sleep with this under your pillow."

"Always the Boy Scout."

"I'm good at my job."

She pulled up the shade and allowed the glow of the snow to lighten the darkness in the room. "Are you okay with this?"

He gave her a nod and blew out the candles before gathering the blankets and settling on the floor. He turned his back to her. She took the opportunity to watch him.

"Good night, Aria."

"Good night, Hawk." She flopped on the bed and rearranged the pillows.

He was good at his job, and reckless about it too. Maybe he had been so reckless because he was so arrogant. Being a firefighter came naturally to him. He couldn't imagine being anything else and had blown a gasket when she asked him to quit. That had been selfish of her and she regretted ever saying it. She had been frightened at the time. He didn't understand that, but here he was giving her a flashlight because he knew how much she hated the dark. He had installed night lights on a timer for her when they lived together. She shook her head. He had been adorable back then. She threw the covers off, but put them back on because the room was drafty. She fluffed the pillow trying to find a good spot to lay her head.

His breathing slowed. He'd probably be snoring

soon. If she didn't fall asleep before him, she'd never get any sleep, and she needed to be fresh in the morning for her bride.

Did he ever think about their good times? When he slept with other women, did he ever wonder about her? She pounded the pillow. She did not want to think about him with someone else. That was too much for her.

"Aria, why don't you give that pillow a break? And me. You're making a racket."

"I'm sorry. I can't get comfortable."

"Try the floor."

But he hadn't moved. She took his silence for acceptance, but hadn't that been one of her mistakes in their marriage? "Are you cold?" she said.

"Only my nose. And my legs. And my arms if I stick them out of the blanket. But don't worry, I'll be fine."

"I could turn up the heat." Her heart yelled to ask him to come to bed to keep them both warm, and her head said to shut up.

"There's no power, sweetheart. There's no heat."

"But the water in the tub was hot."

"Doesn't always work the same way."

His breathing slowed again. He was doing a good job of sleeping even in the cold. Even with her only feet away. He was probably just talking a big talk about competing with Patrick. Hawk probably never gave her much thought. Except he did come to her rescue today. He came to everyone's rescue. Even strangers. Just like he said, he was good at his job.

"Hawk?" She tried to whisper.

"Hmm?"

"Are you asleep?"

"Not if you keep talking to me." Humor lightened his words.

She let out a long breath. "If you stay on your side of the bed, you can share with me." She would not say *sleep with me.* It would hold too many meanings even for her.

"Is that a real invitation?"

"Yes. I feel badly you're sleeping on the floor."

"What will your fiancé say?" He pushed up off the floor and came to the side of the bed.

She could make out his tall silhouette but not the look in his eyes or the curve of his smile. "He doesn't need to know about this."

"Are you sure you want to start your marriage off with a lie?"

She already had. She lied about the piece of her heart that would always belong to Hawk. "Just stay on your side of the bed."

He slid under the covers and turned to face her. There was plenty of space between them, but his oaky scent drifted over and warmed her insides.

"Did you invite me in your bed because it's dark in here?"

"It's too cold for you to sleep on a drafty floor under those windows. This is about survival. And I will admit, I like knowing you're nearby since I don't have my nightlights."

"Have you been back to see your therapist?"

"I have. I'm working on things."

"Does Patrick know?"

She was grateful for the darkness this time. Hawk wouldn't be able to see the blush creeping up her neck. "No."

"If you're going to live with him, you're going to have to tell him."

"I will. Eventually." There had never been a good time to divulge her darkest secrets. Patrick was always busy with work, and when he had a bad day, he needed to unwind. She didn't want to have to explain anyway. No one understood what it was like to have an abusive father unless they did too. Like Hawk.

"Aria, you and I never had secrets."

"No, we just had disappointments."

"Give me a chance to make it up to you." Desperation coated his words.

Her heart ached for his pain and for the man she once loved. She didn't know how to get back to a place where she could trust him. That was her biggest problem. She struggled with trust in all her relationships. To be betrayed by Hawk had been too much.

"Hawk, I —" She inched closer to him. Maybe it was the cold in the room, or maybe her brain had fried from the accident. Maybe it was the wine, even though she only had one glass.

He took her hand in his. "Please, babe. I won't screw up again."

"You've said that before." She should pull away, but she couldn't move.

If she was going to be honest, she had wanted to do this very thing and more.

"I know, but I'm different. I swear. Let me show you." He gripped her hand tighter and rubbed his thumb over her knuckles.

She couldn't do this to Patrick. It wasn't right. And one night in bed would not show her anything except what a tender lover Hawk was, and she already knew that. The bedroom had never been their problem. It would have been easier if it had.

Her life now didn't include Hawk and his antics. She had a good job; she could make her rent; she had a responsible man who seemed to love her very much even if he needed to check on her often. Patrick showed love differently than Hawk. That didn't make it wrong.

"Aria, please give me another chance."

"I'm afraid to." If she gave the rest of her heart to him, and he let her down again, she would not survive another time.

"I know I've said this before, but this time would be different. I'm sober; I'm doing my job again; I'm paying my bills. The only thing missing in my life is you. You don't really love this guy the way you loved me, do you? Does he make you feel the way I did?" His words were a whisper, but she didn't miss their intent.

Heat bloomed between her legs. He always had the power to turn her to a puddle with just a look or a caress. It was no wonder her time in bed with Patrick paled in comparison. His words were stilted and awkward when he approached her for sex. His kisses didn't make her knees weak the way Hawk's did.

She and Hawk were on the brink of something dangerous. If she even took a long breath, it could send her world in a tail spin and yet, if she didn't bridge the space between them and find out what he was offering, she would live her life wondering what if. She could choose to love someone for life, but she could not choose her soulmate.

The storm continued to rage outside, and it matched

the storm between her heart and her head. They were stuck on this island, in this room. She was breaking Patrick's trust. The very thing she found so hard to give to others, and the very thing she expected others to treat with utter care.

"Aria, say something. I'm drowning over here."

"Kiss me."

"Is that what you want?"

"Yes."

"Are you sure?"

She wasn't sure at all. She might be making the biggest mistake of her life, but she couldn't stop herself. For the first time in her life, she was acting before thinking. "Please, kiss me."

CHAPTER FIVE

Hawk reached for Aria and pulled her closer. The warmth of the bed was far better than the cold, hard floor, but because Aria just offered herself to him, not because the mattress was soft and the blankets were made of down.

When he said he wanted to show her how different he was, he meant show her his work in Virginia. Show her his sobriety coins. He was ready to ask his captain for a letter of recommendation. He never expected her to say she wanted to kiss him.

He would only kiss her and nothing more. She was engaged to someone else, and sleeping with another man's woman was the old Hawk. Even if this woman belonged to him first, and clearly she still had feelings for him. He knew her well enough to know her signs. He would not make love to her until that ring was off her finger.

She wrapped her arm around his neck and brought

her soft lips to his, probably tired of waiting for him to make a move. He pushed her mouth open with his tongue. She tasted a little like the wine, and his head spun. Her soft moan made his dick hard. He missed the sounds she made when he touched her.

Her hands ran up his back and curled in his hair. He wanted to touch her everywhere, but he wouldn't. He kept one hand on her hip instead. Their tongues chased each other over and through the ways they knew so well. Kissing her was like going home. She had been the only right thing in his life.

She broke the kiss and placed her lips on his neck, leaving a wet trail on his skin with her tongue. The blood drained from his head. Her hands went under his shirt, and his skin caught fire.

He grabbed her hands. "We can't do this."

"What's the matter?" She scooted away from him and gathered the blankets in her hands.

"I'm not making love to you while you're wearing someone else's ring." This would be the first step to show her he was different.

"I don't understand. I just told you to kiss me."

"Kiss you. Not make love to you and that's what I want to do. If we keep this up, I won't want to stop, and I don't want you to have regrets. You love someone else. I don't want you to hate me in the morning. I think I'd better sleep on the floor."

He forced himself to throw his legs over the side of the bed. He wanted all of her. He wouldn't settle for anything else.

She gripped his arm. "Wait."

She rustled around in the dark and turned on the flashlight. She pointed the light away from him. It casted enough glow to light most of the room.

"The light isn't going to make me change my mind. In fact, I'd rather we make love with the light on. I always liked watching you." He could never get enough of her, and being able to watch her while they made love only made the sex hotter.

"Are you watching now?"

"Yeah."

She slid her ring off and held it up for him to see. A knot formed in his throat. She opened the bedside table drawer and placed it in there.

"If someone told me this morning, I would be making love to my ex-husband tonight, I would have laughed. But being with you today, the way you've taken care of me in the storm, has forced me to admit out loud I'm not over you. I've never been able to let you go completely. I do care deeply for Patrick, but he's not you. I can't promise you anything except tonight. If you can handle that, then I'm willing to try."

"To try what?" His heart picked up speed. He didn't want to hope too much.

"To try to trust you." Her words were a whisper, but he caught every one.

He cupped her face in his shaking hands. "I'll show you I'm worth it. Not just tonight. I will do whatever it takes to prove to you I'm worthy of you."

"Complete trust will take some time. Are you willing to wait it out?"

"Yes." He'd wait forever for her.

"And you'll be honest with me?"

"Completely."

"Make love to me, Hawk Egan."

CHAPTER SIX

This was crazy. Aria couldn't believe she just took off her engagement ring without a thought and stuck it in a drawer, but the moment Hawk slid into the bed beside her she knew. All she wanted was to kiss him. Her skin tingled to be touched by him, to feel him inside her. She had to control herself not to tear his clothes off. She never felt that way with Patrick. The call to Patrick was to end their relationship. He deserved to be with someone who loved him with their whole heart. It wasn't her. Her heart still belonged to Hawk.

Hawk pushed a piece of hair away from her face. "This isn't a dream, right? I'm not going to wake up on that floor and this never happened?"

She dropped the blankets and unzipped her hoodie. She only had on a tank top underneath. The cool air of the room made her nipples hard. She took his hand and covered her breast with it. "This is as real as it gets."

"I'll treat you right." He kissed her neck, and she forgot about everything else.

It had been so long since sex had been charged with electricity. She couldn't wait. She needed to feel all of him. Her hands pulled at his shirt until he let her go and yanked it over his head. Her lips were on his again. Her tongue tangled with his, and it wasn't enough. She pushed at his shorts so she could get her hands inside his boxer briefs. Her fingers dragged over the taut muscles of his legs.

His touch drove her to the edge. His hand was on her breast rubbing the nipple between his fingers. He moved his hand down her belly and cupped her bottom. His erection pressed against her. She wasn't going to be able to wait.

"Let me get out of these." She dragged the sweats over her legs and tossed them to the side.

His hand was inside her panties, but he didn't touch the place she most wanted him to. That was okay; she needed to taste him before they went any further. She pushed him back on the bed and ran her tongue over the muscles in his chest. Her fingers played with his soft chest hair.

He gripped her hand and sucked on her fingers. She gasped and gazed up at him through her lashes. Her breath came in short spurts.

"You are beautiful, babe."

She smiled but didn't lift her mouth from his skin. Instead, she nipped a little on her way down his side until she ran into his underwear. She gripped them between her teeth and dragged them over his legs.

"That's new." Hawk laughed, but he wasn't making fun.

He would never make fun of her. She had told him

her worst secret, and he had not judged her. She should have paid him the same respect when he told her about his alcohol abuse. She pushed those thoughts away. She didn't want to be reminded of their past as she was about to take him in her mouth.

Her tongue ran over his hip. He tasted salty and sweet. Like heaven.

"Hold on." He sat up.

"You don't like what I'm doing?" She was being too aggressive. She had never been like this with him in quite this way.

"The exact opposite. Come here." He pulled her to him. "This is a little embarrassing, but you wanted honesty."

She thought she did. "Is it bad?"

He laughed. "Only for me. I haven't been with anyone in a while. I don't think I'll be able to hold out if you wrap your lips around me."

"That's it? Who cares? We can do it again."

"Babe, I might only get one chance. In the light of day, no matter what you said tonight, you could send me packing. I'm better, but I'm still me, and that might not suit you. I want to feel your legs around my hips, and I want us to come together. Okay?"

His words stole her breath. She wanted to say she still loved him for his tenderness, but she bit the words back. Instead, she slid back on the pillows and guided him above her. "How's this?"

"One more thing." He jumped up and grabbed his duffle bag. He returned with a condom and had it on in seconds.

She reached over and turned off the flashlight. The

darkness didn't bother her when it was just her and Hawk. No one in the outside world could get to her. Not with him around. "Being in the dark is good practice for me."

"Whatever you want. Lights on. Lights off. The floor. The bed. You could tie me to the bed. I don't care as long as it's us."

The delicious laughter slipped over her tongue. "We could arrange for a little tying up."

He slid inside her, filling her, and she wrapped her legs around his hips. They rocked in a slow steady rhythm, but the urgency returned, and she grinded her hips to meet his.

Desire coiled with each thrust. She needed more and gripped his butt to push him further. His lips found her breast again, and she soared until her muscles clenched, and the wild, sweet explosion she never had with another man shook her.

He let go and growled out her name. She wrapped her arms around him to hold him close while their hearts slowed. He rolled to his side and took her with him.

She didn't say a word. She didn't want the magic to end. He was right. In the light of day, she might panic and change her mind. He had cheated on her. He had lied to her. He drank too much and almost died the night his brother did. He knew how hard it was for her to trust, and he had disintegrated that.

Tears pricked the back of her eyes. What had she done to her life by putting Hawk back in it? What if he couldn't keep his promises this time? Would a passion-less life with an awkward, but reliable man be better than a life full of passion and love with a man who had the power to destroy her heart?

The storm continued to blow outside, shaking the windows in their sills while the storm inside her raged. She had just acted no better than her father.

Her father had broken her heart a long time ago with his lies. She swore she'd never let that kind of pain happen again, but Hawk had hurt her. Hawk had also loved her with the same fierceness he showed when he saved lives. As long as that storm stuck around and the bridge remained up, she would be all right. But when it was time to go back to the real world, could she do it with him?

He gathered the blankets around them and kissed her head. "You okay?"

"Never better."

She had asked for honesty.

Now she was lying.

CHAPTER SEVEN

Hawk rolled over and reached for Aria. His hand landed on a piece of hotel stationery. He pushed up and ran a hand over his face to get the sleep out of his eyes. He blinked a few times before her flowing script came into view.

Good morning. I had some work to do so I let you sleep. Thank you for last night. A.

He climbed out of bed and put the note in his duffle. Last night had been a complete surprise. One he wasn't about to let go of. He planned on keeping Aria in his bed permanently.

He checked the drawer in the side table. The ring was gone. He groaned, but it didn't mean she was wearing it. She could've put it in her luggage. He eyed the suitcase but resisted the urge to rummage through it. He wasn't that guy anymore. She had to trust him again, or they would never make it. Trust was the most important thing to her, and he had ruined it. The fact that she might give him another chance blew his mind.

He turned on the shower and hoped for some hot water. He flipped the light switch, and the lights on the wall flanking the mirror came to life. The hot water steamed up the glass shower door. He stepped inside.

What if she wouldn't give him another chance? Maybe last night was more about one for the road than a relationship with him. They had always been good in bed together. It could have been a last hurrah before married life. It wasn't her style to use him. It wasn't her style to betray someone either, but she tore that ring off without hesitation. He wouldn't lie, that move beefed up his pride. Old Patrick could stick it. Aria wanted him.

He dried off, got dressed, and shoved his phone in his pocket. He went looking for her. The lobby bustled with people. Some sat on rocking chairs engrossed in their phones. Others carried coffee cups as they moved from one room to the next lost in conversation. The couple from the front desk, Ethan and Mike, gave him a wave from the sofa by the fireplace.

The storm continued outside. They had a couple of feet of snow already. The skies were still gray. He found Henry standing behind the front desk. "How's it going, Henry?"

"Fine, sir. Did you have a pleasurable night?"

He tried not to smirk. "I did indeed. Any word on the bridge?" He still hoped to make it to Virginia before the weekend was over.

"It's still in the up position, I'm afraid. But our generators are working. Most of the hotel is operational. Except the ballroom area."

"Which way is that again?" It had been pretty dark in

there last night when he helped Aria bring her boxes in. That seemed like a lifetime ago.

"Through the Brown Lounge." Henry pointed over Hawk's shoulder.

He went through the room decorated in brown until the sound of yelling met him half way. Aria stood in the middle of the ballroom waving her arms. She was beautiful when she got fired up like that. Her green eyes darkened like the surface of a lake at dusk. Sometimes when they fought, and the color of her eyes changed, he'd only want to make love to her. She usually got mad because he was distracting her with sex, but it was because her strong personality was such a turn on. He was also a lot younger and had better stamina back then.

A young man in the standard hotel uniform of white shirt and black vest stood there with his head hung while Aria continued to pummel him with questions the poor kid couldn't answer.

"We can't have a wedding in here for two hundred and fifty people if the generators aren't working," she said.

"I can check, ma'am." The kid hurried off before Aria could hand him his head.

"Ugh." She threw her hands in the air again.

"Everything okay?" He wanted to go to her and wrap her in his arms, but he would let her make the move.

She spun at the sound of his voice. "Do you know how to fix a generator?"

"Not unless it's been on a firetruck."

"The lights aren't working in here and neither are any of the outlets which means the band can't plug in their speakers or instruments. Hey, what about extension cords?" She snapped her fingers. The ring was missing.

"Since the outlets in here aren't working, you'd have to run the cords through the doorway, ceiling or floor. Can't let you do that. Fire hazard."

"Ooh. You're no fun."

"A fire would be less fun. You still have a day. The power might come back on."

She came toward him. The tightness in his chest eased. She wasn't getting rid of him just yet. "The bridge is still up. None of the vendors can get here. That's a problem. I'm having twenty-five tall glass vases delivered today. The flowers are supposed to arrive tomorrow. And the worst part is the groom can't get here."

He took a tentative step closer. "Only worry about the things you can control."

"I'm supposed to be controlling every aspect of this wedding. If this bride is pleased, she could send me a lot of clients. I need this to work out." She hooked her fingers through his belt loops and tugged.

Heat ran over his skin. He brushed a strand of her hair from her face. "It will all work out. You'll see."

"Easy for you to say. You sit around a firehouse all day, play cards with the guys, and collect a paycheck." Her lip curled up, and the glint in her eyes teased him.

"Are you busting my hump, lady?" He cupped her bottom and pulled her against him.

She ran her hands over his chest. "Your hump needs a little busting sometimes." She shoved him with a laugh. "In all seriousness, I want this wedding to work out."

He gathered her in his arms and rested his chin on

her head. "You're going to make it special. I have no doubt."

"Thank you for saying that." She eased away and met his gaze. "You know I was joking about your job, right? I'm proud of what you do for a living."

Heat ran up his neck. Her words eased the weight of doubt he carried around. He wanted to be enough for her, and that included his job. She had wanted him to be something else once. "I'm glad you changed your mind about my being a firefighter."

"I'm sorry I ever said those words."

He wanted the lightness in her eyes back. "But I don't play cards." He tapped her nose.

"That's because you always stunk at cards." She laughed and escaped his grasp.

"Hey, come back here." He lunged for her, but missed.

"I need to check on my car." She waved her phone.

"Aria," a female called from behind him.

"Celine." Aria walked past him with her shoulders back and her face arranged in a neutral expression. The phone was now in her back pocket.

Whoever this Celine was, she just ruined a perfectly good mood. He had wanted to ask Aria to grab some breakfast with him. Maybe convince her to come back to the hotel room. If they were stuck at the hotel, and the storm was still going, they might as well make the most of their time together.

He strode up beside Aria.

"I'm working on a solution. If the vendors can't make it to the island, we'll improvise," Aria said.

"But what if my pastor can't get here? And Ken? I

can't get married without my fiancé." Celine dabbed at her eyes.

Aria grabbed her hands. "Let's not panic. We'll find a way to get him here. This storm can't last forever. In the meantime, enjoy your time with your bridesmaids. Do you have dinner reservations in the restaurant for tonight?"

"I hadn't thought about that."

"I'll take care of it. I'll make it for six tonight in your name."

She was handling this chick pretty well. He was proud of her. She had built a business in the midst of getting divorced, and he hadn't made the break up easy. Celine had herself a big sniffle and threw her arms around Aria. Aria blinked, but patted Celine's back.

"You are the best wedding planner, ever. I'm going to tell all my friends about you."

"Thank you. There is one more thing. I was in a car accident on my way here, and some of the favors broke. I don't think we'll have enough for everyone."

"Oh, no. Those were so special and went with my theme. I'm disappointed. I can't have a completely set table without enough favors. And what will the guests say who came if they don't get a little present from the bride and groom?"

"And she's okay. Thanks for asking," he said.

Aria shot him a death glare. He shrugged and shoved his hands in his pockets.

Celine fanned her face with her hands. "Oh, I'm so sorry. Forgive me and my bad manners. I should've asked if you were all right. That's what really matters. Not the favors. The bridal party doesn't need them, and if that's still not enough, I'll just order more and ship them to the guests at their homes."

"That's a great idea," Aria said.

"I'm really blundering today. I'm Celine Wood. You must be Aria's handsome fiancé." Celine stuck out her hand.

He shook. "I'm Hawk. It's nice to meet you. I have to make a call. I'll see you later, babe." He planted a kiss on Aria's lips before she could say anything and walked out.

She was going to be pissed about that, but in a way he saved her from having to explain who he was. Since she wasn't wearing the ring this morning, she might be rethinking the fiancé thing.

A hallway off the lobby offered a gift store, the spa, and a small café. The café had large windows that faced the ocean. Book shelves were in-between the windows. It was like a mini bookstore inside the store. He perused the titles and picked up a thriller.

"Can I have a large coffee and one of those muffins?" He pointed to the glass case beside the counter. "And the book too."

A woman with mocha skin and hair as dark as night smiled at him. "Of course. Are you enjoying your stay at the Horseman?" She grabbed a cup and started pouring.

"So far so good. Looks like you have power in here." The coffee machines gurgled. The lights were on, and the temperature in the room felt comfortable.

"This part of the hotel is newer. The generator is bigger and newer too."

"Did only the hotel lose power?"

"The whole section along the south beach. Many homes are still without power. I'm one of them. I walked to work today to avoid the traffic lights that are out." She handed him the coffee and the muffin. "That will be twenty-seven with the book. Are you here on business?"

"The storm detoured me." He fished his wallet out of his jeans and handed over the money.

"Are you traveling alone?" She leaned on the counter and flashed a very bright smile.

"Not exactly."

"A few of us are staying over in the hotel tonight. We're going to meet up at the club in the basement, if you're looking for something to do." She hit a few buttons on the register and the paper receipt rolled out. She tore it off and wrote on it. "That's my cell. No pressure. I just thought if you're bored, and that book ends up not holding your interest, you might want to come out. Since you're alone."

His hand hesitated above the paper. He'd rather stay in and in bed, but Aria might like a night out. The beautiful lady behind the counter turned over his hand and placed her number in his palm. She closed his grip and left her hand on his. His brain took a second to catch up. He tried to pull away, but she held on and flashed her bright smile again.

"Hawk?"

He spun at the sound of his name. Aria glared at him with a crease between her brows. She had heard most of the conversation. The woman behind the counter returned to making coffee. She had taken the phone number with her.

"Hey." He wanted to ease the worry from her face and stepped forward. She moved back. "Aria, it's not what you think."

"It never is." She turned and was gone.

She was so stupid. They had barely slept together five minutes ago, and he was flirting with another woman, telling her he was alone in the hotel and available, and not just that, but he embarrassed her in front of Celine with that flippant comment. Aria pushed through the door and went out the back to the grassy area that faced the ocean.

The snow still fell, but the wind had died down some. She pressed against the brick to keep from getting soaked. She didn't have on a coat and wasn't about to go inside and get one. She needed to get away from him, to breathe some fresh air before she puked.

She glanced at her left hand. Her whole life was ruined now. She could never control herself around Hawk, and she could never tell him no. It wasn't his fault that they slept together. She knew exactly what she wanted last night. He had a way of making her toss aside reason, and that didn't work for her. He was the impulsive one, the careless one. Not her. She needed to stick to her plan, and that didn't involve Hawk Egan.

She let out a long breath. He had been so sweet to her last night. It was one of the reason's she loved him so much. He was gentle, caring and generous with her.

"No." She banged her fists against her leg.

"Ma'am, everything all right?"

She hadn't heard the man approach. "I'm fine. I just needed some air. Thanks."

"Name's John." He stuck out his hand. In the other was a shovel.

He was short and bald. His eyes twinkled, and his cheeks were rosy. His smile was warm and welcoming. She found herself shaking hands with him, when any other time she would have told a stranger like him to go away.

"I'm Aria."

"Well, Aria, it's a bit cold out here without a coat."

"What are you doing outside then?"

"I work here. I'm the gardener. Not much work in January, but I keep up with the grounds. We're salting and shoveling the sidewalks around the hotel so you can come outside for fresh air." He chuckled, and his whole body shook.

The tension slid from her shoulders. "You remind me of someone."

"I get that a lot. I think it's Santa Claus." He patted his belly and laughed again.

"I think it's someone else." Maybe her grandfather. He had been a sweet man whose face lit up when she walked into the room. He died when she was young, and could have used him around to ward off her father.

"Does something have you all tied up in knots?"

She rubbed her arms for warmth. "What makes you say that?"

"You came barreling out of that door like someone was chasing you."

Her past was chasing her. "I think I saw something I didn't like."

"You think or you know?"

"I don't know. I might have jumped to conclusions. I reacted based on past knowledge."

"Can you gather more information?" He leaned on the shovel.

The snow cascaded down and dusted his bald head. He didn't even seem to notice. The sense of peace lulled her. Her eyelids wanted to close.

"I could ask some questions," she said.

"Then that sounds exactly like what you should do. Now, let's get inside. This storm is burrowing into my old bones. I swear I'm moving to Florida one of these days and live with my granddaughter."

"Thank you for talking with me." She stepped inside, and he followed.

"My pleasure."

She turned into the brown room. "Can I buy you a cup of coffee since I kept you outside so long?"

He didn't respond.

She turned to see that he had disappeared.

"Strange."

She had overreacted when it came to Hawk. It was an old habit. That woman was flirting with him; she had heard part of the conversation. She couldn't blame him for being attractive to women. He was very sexy, but in the past he had strayed. Twice. Both times he was drunk and the second was the day Wyatt died. They had been fighting so much by then, she wasn't surprised he found comfort with another woman. She certainly wasn't giving any comfort to him back then.

She searched the lobby, the coffee shop, the restaurant, and the club in the basement. She couldn't find him. She hadn't bothered to charge her phone this morning.

She had wanted to get out of the room before he woke up, and if she was going to be honest, she wasn't ready to speak with Patrick. She would before the weekend ended, but just not right now. Now she wanted to find Hawk and apologize.

CHAPTER EIGHT

Hawk was the only one out on the street. The snow piled up on the cobblestone walkway and blew in drifts up against the front doors of all the stores on the promenade. He had to march to get down the street because the snow came up to his ankles.

Fire burned in his veins. How could Aria think he was coming onto that woman only hours after they made love? She was never going to trust him. He was wasting his time trying to win her over. She was always going to think he was shit.

He pulled out his phone and dialed Phoenix. He needed someone in his corner for a little while.

"Hey, man, how's the storm? Can you get down here?" his brother's voice came across the line.

"The snow has lightened up for now. The bridge is still stuck. I can't get off yet. How's it going?"

"The grief retreat is great. The participants are actually doing the activities. When they don't realize they're working through their grief, they accomplish something.

You're a genius. Hang on a second." Phoenix moved the phone which made rustling sounds as if he had covered the microphone. "Sorry. I'm back."

"I'm glad things are going well." He wanted to be there. Helping others work through their grief helped him continue to work through his. "Can you handle the whole thing by yourself?"

"Shit, yeah, baby brother." Phoenix laughed. "Anything else going on?"

"Nothing but the snow."

"Not even with Aria?" Phoenix's question stopped him in his tracks.

"How do you know that?" He had no plans to discuss his love life with anyone until he had more questions answered.

"You weren't the only one who heard the police scanner. I hoped you would stay away from her. Where is she?"

"What difference does that make?" He started walking again.

"It makes a huge difference if you're tangling with her," Phoenix said.

"She's stuck on the island too." There was no point in lying to his brother.

The road came to an intersection. On the corner was an old brick firehouse. Cape May Station 1. The place looked dark on the inside. He tried the door, but it was locked.

"And that means you can't stay away from her. When are you going to learn? She's not right for you."

When things went sour with Aria, Phoenix had taken his side even though he was mostly at fault. Phoenix didn't know he had broken his vows and slept with someone that night.

"Phoenix, don't lecture me right now. I can handle Aria." He wanted to ask his older brother whether he believed in soulmates or not, but the words got stuck in his throat. Phoenix would give him shit for talking like that anyway.

"Like hell you can."

"I didn't call you so you can give me shit. You could try to have my back on this one."

He cupped his hand over his eyes and tried to get a better look inside the firehouse. There were only two trucks and no movement. It was a volunteer squad unlike his where everyone was on the books, and the station was manned twenty-four seven.

"I do have your back. That's why I don't want you involved with her. After the way she treated you the night Wyatt died, I've got nothing for her."

He wiped a hand over his face. "Everyone was upset that night. We all made mistakes." Especially him. He and Aria had fought when he called her. She hadn't even given him a chance to tell her what happened. He had found solace in someone else's arms that night.

"Where has she been the past two years?"

"Phoenix, enough. I don't want to talk about Aria anymore." The fire that had burned in his veins when he started this walk only burned hotter now. He clenched his fists wanting to hit something. He hoped Phoenix would understand with Aria in his life, the wounds would close and he'd be happy again.

"I don't want you to start drinking again. I can't lose two brothers."

He had been extremely drunk the night Wyatt died. He couldn't see straight. The pain had been unbearable because Wyatt wasn't just his brother. Wyatt was his hero. His problems always came back to his drinking. He had hurt everyone he loved and was sorrier than they knew.

"I won't let that happen. I have too much to stay sober for."

"Stay away from Aria. Promise me."

"I don't know." He wouldn't make that promise. Not after what happened between them.

"Did you sleep with her?"

"I said enough of this conversation. If you can't support me, then shut the hell up."

"You want her to give you another chance, don't you?" Phoenix's questions were like a smoke filled room without a way out.

"What if she would give me a second chance? Would it be so bad for me to find a little happiness? She's the best thing that ever happened to me."

If he could rewind history, he would go back to the night Wyatt died and make different choices that would save his marriage.

"You're acting like a fool. I'm so glad I don't fall in love. It's got you all turned around. Always has. I'm putting it on the record you two should stay away from each other."

"Duly noted. I've got to go." He should try and find the chief of the station and ask if he could bunk here until the storm passed.

"Hawk, man, don't be mad."

"I said I had to go. I'll call you when the bridge is

down." He ended the call and shoved his phone back in his pocket.

Phoenix didn't understand how he much Aria meant to him. Aria didn't seem to understand how he felt about her either if she could so easily believe the worst of him. It was easier to believe the bad stuff.

The wet snow soaked his legs. His jeans started starting to stick to him, and his toes were numb. He needed to turn back and warm up. Maybe he'd stop in that coffee shop and take the pretty lady up on her offer. Aria was expecting him to do it anyway. She didn't believe he could change.

Maybe he couldn't. His father never changed. Why should he be any different?

Aria gave up. She couldn't find Hawk anywhere in the hotel. His duffle was still in the room, and his truck was still in the parking lot. That was a good sign. But he was probably mad at her for the way she reacted, and when he got mad, he didn't always think straight.

She kicked off her shoes and flopped on the bed. No deliveries came today for the wedding, which put her behind schedule. First thing tomorrow, she planned on scavenging anything she could find to create the decorations for the ballroom. If the bridge didn't start working, not even the groom would be here. Maybe they could get married over video chat. She chuckled at her bad idea.

A novel on the table caught her attention. It hadn't been there earlier. Hawk must've bought it this morning. Her fingers traced the raised title. A thriller, his favorite kind. He used to read in bed before he went to sleep. She would climb in beside him and snuggle against him, forcing him to wrap his arm around her. She could always manage to get him to put the book down and make love to her. She let out a long breath. She missed him.

She plugged her phone in to charge. Patrick had left two messages wondering where she was. He was worried about her, which was sweet, but she detected an edge to his voice. Or that was her guilt talking. She owed him an explanation, but not until she made sure Hawk was okay. Patrick would be fine working his financial deals and hanging with his college buddies this weekend. He certainly didn't need her. Hawk, on the other hand, had needed her more than once, and she had let him down.

She still wanted to be sick when she thought about the night Wyatt died, and he called her for help. She hadn't given him a chance to speak. She just screamed at him because of the bills. She had behaved deplorably and yet right in this bed, he asked her to give him another try. She should be asking him for forgiveness for her past behavior.

The lock in the hotel room door jiggled. Her heart raced. Hawk came through the entryway. His hair was wet, and his teeth were chattering.

"Oh my God, were you outside in the snow without a hat?" She jumped from the bed.

"I'm fine." He put his hands up to stop her.

"Your lips are blue, and your pants are all wet. You need to get out of them." She ran for a towel.

"Aria, I don't need your help." He called after her.

She stood in the doorway clutching the towel to her chest. Anger twisted his face into a scowl.

"I know you're mad, but you could have hypothermia. Please, Hawk, take off those clothes." She would give him the space he needed to calm down, then she could try and talk to him about what happened earlier.

"I don't have hypothermia." He swiped the towel and dried at his hair. He removed his boots and peeled off his jeans.

She averted her gaze. In the light of day, even though it was still snowing, seeing him in his underwear caused heat to run up her neck and face.

He shoved his long, muscular legs into a pair of sweats and sat on the bed. "We need to talk," he said.

"I'm sorry." She wanted to get it out first. If he couldn't forgive her, that would be okay. She spent the past two years without him. She'd be fine alone.

"You are?" He narrowed his eyes.

"Don't act so surprised." She sat beside him. "I'm still afraid, and I don't know if I ever won't be. I saw that woman in the coffee shop smiling at you that way women do when they want to climb on top of a man and your hands linked, and I panicked. She was young and pretty, and we're nothing to each other."

He slid his cold fingers through hers. She rubbed her other hand over his to get some warmth going in his skin.

"I want us to be everything to each other again, but I need you to believe in me just a little. If you can't do that, then I don't think we'll have a future."

Her breath caught. She couldn't imagine a future that didn't include Hawk. How could she walk this world and never speak to him again? And how did she learn to trust him?

"Can I ask you something?"

"Ask me anything. I'm an open book," he said.

"Have you slept with a lot of women since me?" She understood why he wanted to know about Patrick. If she were going to give him another chance, she wanted to know who she competed with too.

"Babe, you want me to be honest?"

"Yes."

"There have been some women, sure, but I have never felt for another woman the way I feel about you. My turn to ask a question. Have you spoken to your fiancé about us yet?"

"I will."

He pulled his hand away. "Does that mean you're regretting last night?"

"No, of course not."

"You know, my having sex with someone isn't the same as you getting engaged. I could never make a commitment to another woman because she wasn't you. Did I mean nothing to you?"

He'd been her whole world. That was why his betrayal and his drinking hurt so much she couldn't breathe. "I wasn't trying to spite you by getting engaged. I thought I knew what I wanted."

"And now you don't?"

"I don't want Patrick anymore." She met his gaze.

"But you don't want me either?" Pain passed over his eyes.

She wanted to ease the crease between his brows. "Hawk, give me time, please."

He went to the window and turned his back to her. She told her feet to stay still. Her mind needed the time to weigh out what she was doing here, but her heart kicked her brain to the curb and forced her feet forward.

She wrapped her arms around his waist and rested her cheek on his back. She closed her eyes and relaxed against the intake of his breath.

"I'm in this for long haul, Aria. I don't want a one-night thing with you. I'll wait for you." He linked his arms with hers.

"Thank you."

"So, tell me more about this look." He eased out of her grip and turned to face her. A mischievous smile tugged at his lips.

"What look is that?"

"The one women give when they want to climb on top of a man. I don't think I've seen it."

Laughter bubbled up inside her and popped out. "Did I say that?"

"Yup. When you were talking about the woman in the coffee shop. You thought she wanted to climb on top of me because of the look on her face. Can you explain that to me?" He wagged his eyebrows.

She flopped back on the bed. "You've seen it. You just don't know because you aren't paying attention."

"Have you given this look to Patrick?" He slid on the bed beside her.

She doubted it. There had been plenty of times she faked sleeping to get out of sex with Patrick. She blamed it on being tired or having a rough day. How could she have ever thought she would be able to spend her entire life with a man who thought her on top was kinky?

Because she believed marrying the bad boy was a mistake.

"Never mind Patrick. Are you any warmer? I could get you some coffee."

"I want to see this look." The playful and mischievous grin tugged on his lips again.

"I'm afraid, Lieutenant Egan, you will just have to wait for that one. Let's get some coffee." She stood and tugged her shirt into place.

"What did you say?" He narrowed his eyes.

"What do you mean?" Had she said something she shouldn't have?

"You know I got promoted." He climbed off the bed and closed the space between them.

So she had. She had searched his name countless times on the internet to make sure he hadn't been hurt in a fire. She followed the police blotter of his town to see where fires broke out. His promotion had made the town's paper. Her chest had filled with pride for him. When she saw the picture of him standing there in his uniform, she had cried.

"I saw it somewhere."

He cupped her face between his calloused hands and placed a tender kiss on her lips. The current between them scorched her from the inside out. A tender kiss wouldn't be enough. She had been hungry for this all-encompassing affection.

She wrapped her arms around his neck and curled her fingers in his damp hair. She loved the longer, silky strands. He pushed her lips apart with his tongue. He tasted minty like he had been chewing gum.

She pressed against him. The need inside grew

stronger. She grinded her hips against him, and he slid his thigh between her legs. Her breath caught, but she moved to the rhythm he set with his leg. Her frenzied hands tugged at the waistband of his sweatpants. He undid her pants and lifted her up never breaking their kiss.

She wrapped her legs around him, and he backed her against the wall. The picture beside her shook. He thrust inside her, and her muscles clenched around him as he drove into her again and again. There was nothing else in that moment except the heat between them. She rode the wave of sheer pleasure until it crashed, tossing and turning her until she was spent.

He met her there with his chest heaving and his breath labored. His heart beat in the same frantic rhythm that hers did.

She traced the line of his jaw dusted in day old beard. "You take my breath away."

He eased away and guided them to the bed. They lay facing each other, but she had to touch him.

"I don't want anyone else. Tell me when this storm is over and we have to go back to real life, you won't walk away from me again." He brushed her sweaty hair from her face.

There was still so much to figure out. She didn't want to make promises she couldn't keep. She would need time to see what he was really like now, but what they shared in this room would count because no one else could make her feel this way. That had to be more than just sex.

She opened her mouth to tell him she wanted to take

a chance, but take it slow. The ringing of her phone stopped her.

"Don't get that," he said.

"But it could be Celine. I'll just look."

He flopped on his back. She leaned over him to grab her phone on the table. Her hand hovered.

"Well?"

"It's not Celine. It's Patrick."

CHAPTER NINE

"You'd better get that." Hawk reassembled his sweatpants and pushed off the bed. A darkness passed over his eyes.

She couldn't talk to Patrick minutes after making love to Hawk. That wasn't fair to either man. "Stay. I'll talk to him later, but I do need to speak with him." No matter what happened between her and Hawk, her relationship with Patrick wasn't right. She dropped the phone back on the table and held a hand out to Hawk.

He jumped back on the bed. The impish grin had returned to its rightful place. "Are you going to end it with him?"

"I don't think he loved me the right way." His constant hovering was sweet at first, but after a while it seemed more like insecurity.

"Then why did you get engaged?"

"Because he wasn't you."

"Ouch."

"By the time things ended between us I thought if I

ever became involved with another man he would have to be the opposite of you."

"How'd that work out?"

She went to the window. The cold air drifted in from the sides of the glass, and the snow continued to paint the island in strokes of white. It would take some time to dig out of this mess.

"What's happening here is wonderful, but it's not real life." Guilt sat heavy on her chest. She wanted to keep parts of her life separate, and the storm could allow that for a little while, but by Monday she'd have to face her choices.

"It's real life to me." He grabbed her shoulder and turned her to face him. Pain deepened the lines around his mouth. Her heart hallowed out.

"Don't you want to see how we are together after a long day at work, or when one of us is sick, or just in a bad mood?" She missed his touch but didn't reach out to him.

"What you're saying is you want to find out if I still go off halfcocked in those situations."

"Can you blame me?"

"Why are you sleeping with me? Do you need to get something out of your system? Another go-'round with the ex because he knows how to bring you to a climax."

Was that what she was doing because her sex life had been less than stellar? If he hadn't shown up to help her in the storm, would she have even considered calling him for another try? Fear would have paralyzed her from taking the risk. As long as she kept her distance, she would never jeopardize her heart where he was concerned. He had hurt her enough, and she believed to some degree if he really loved her, he wouldn't have done the things he did.

"Your silence says that must be it. If you hurry, you can catch your fiancé. You don't even have to tell him about us if you want to keep another secret from him. I certainly won't give you away. At least you can never accuse me of that. And whatever this thing was between us, it's over because I told you. I'm not interested in an affair." He reached for the door.

"Hawk, wait."

He stormed out and slammed the door shut.

She dropped onto the window seat and held her head in her hands. He had every right to be mad at her. She didn't want to make promises, but he did. He always promised her one thing or another, but when his drinking got worse, he couldn't keep them. She didn't know how to stop holding that over his head.

If she was someone else, maybe she'd feel differently. But she was the girl whose father locked her in the closet to punish her. He kept her sisters from her when she cried, and every time she asked him for anything, he attached a price to it she couldn't pay. She didn't know how to trust the right way.

But it had been Hawk who had helped her with that. He brought her into the light just enough she had hope. The tears spilled over her fingers and dripped on her legs. Since their divorce, she'd been in the dark again. These past two days had put her on the road home. She wished he could wait for her this time, but she had hurt him too.

She wiped her nose with the back of her hand. He couldn't have gone far. Hopefully, he didn't find his way to the bar. She stopped with the room key in her hand. She would need to stop thinking that way if she was going to make a life with him. He'd been sober a long time, but what if something happened that threatened that sobriety. Would he fall? Or would someone else die?

Her phone vibrated with a text. She should ignore it and go after Hawk. Unless it was him. She glanced at the screen and swallowed the disappointment as she read Celine's name.

Ken wants to call off the wedding
Because of the weather?
Forever

Her stomach twisted into a braid. Ken couldn't want out of the wedding. These two seemed so perfect for each other. She dialed Celine's cell. This wasn't a conversation to have via text. Celine picked up and said hello through tears.

"Celine, are you sure? Did he say why?"

Celine blew her nose. "He said the weather was a sign. He'd been debating this decision for weeks. It's two days before our wedding. How can he do this?"

"It might just be cold feet. Do you want me to call him?" Part of her job as a wedding planner was being a therapist for those about to walk down the aisle. There had been a few brides and grooms who panicked at the last second. She never really understood the thought to back out until Patrick started pushing her to set the date.

"Would you? I told him I didn't care about the big wedding. I just want to be married to him. We can call off this circus. It was all my mother's idea anyway. Now the storm has made it all but impossible to pull it off."

Her chance of planning future weddings for Celine's

crowd melted away like snowflakes in the sun. If Celine called off the big event, no one would see the magic she had created for the bride and groom. Her business really needed this shot.

"If I can talk to Ken, will you consider still having the wedding?"

"How are we going to have a big wedding when the only people who are here are me, my bridesmaids, and you?"

"The bridge could still work. Like you said, we have two days."

"Oh, whatever. If Ken agrees, then I do too. Let me know what he says." Celine ended the call.

She should go after Hawk first. Her phone vibrated in her hand. With some hesitation, she peeked at the screen. "Hey, Mack."

"Hi. How are you? I was so worried with this weather."

"I'm fine. I've been stuck on the island. I'm hoping the wedding is still a go." If she could convince Ken not to end things before they'd even begun. "What's going on?"

"David is fighting me for custody. That bastard. He knows I can't afford a good lawyer. He wants to take the boys and live out of state."

"He can't do that."

"Damn straight he can't. I'll kill him in his sleep first."

"Mack, don't talk like that."

"You might be the sister that avoids confrontation, but that's not me, and you know it. What Dad did to us only made me angry and looking for a fight. If David wants a fight, he's going to get one."

"Whatever you need, I'm here for you."

"Thanks. Let's talk about something else. How's Patrick?"

She took a deep breath. "I have something to tell you." She told her sister about the accident, Hawk, and her decision to end her engagement.

"Are you crazy? You can't get back together with Hawk. He's trouble, and he's going to bring you a ton of trouble. I'm just glad you two never had kids. At least you can walk away from him and not be tied to him forever like me and David. Please, walk away from him."

Aria placed a hand on her belly. They may have made a baby. She was still young enough. They would just be older parents, if Hawk was even okay with the idea of children. They had never talked about kids. With both of their checkered pasts, and their poor parenting role models, maybe being parents together could really screw a kid up. It would be better for now if their one time without a condom didn't result in a baby.

"I love him, Mack. I can't give up on him. Give him a chance, for me." If Hawk even still wanted her.

"God, he always had a way of turning you upside down. I think this is a bad idea, but if you want to be with him, I can't stop you."

"Will you try and support me? And be nice to him when you see him?"

"I'll support you because I love you, but do I have to be nice to him?" Mack laced her words with sarcastic humor.

"It won't hurt you to be nice to someone else."

"Hey, I'm nice. Most of the time."

She laughed. "Promise me you won't bite his head off when you see him."

"Okay, okay. I promise. But if he hurts you again, I'm going to hunt him down. Just so we're clear."

"That's fine. I should run. I need to call a client." And save a wedding.

"Good luck." Mack ended the call.

Her fingers tapped away at her phone screen and pulled up Ken's number. She hit the button and held her breath.

"Ken Richards."

"Ken, it's Aria. Celine just called me. Are you sure you want to end things?"

"Look, I'm sorry about your fee and all. I can make sure you still get paid for the work you did, but I don't want to get married."

"I'm not calling about my fee. You two are a great couple. It's normal to get cold feet right before." She ran her hands over Hawk's wet jeans. They had eloped. He had whisked her away to Washington State and a sweet little inn where they stood by a waterfall and exchanged unplanned vows.

"I don't have cold feet. I can't trust her."

"Excuse me?"

"She's horrible with money. She spent a fortune decorating our new house and didn't tell me. When I found out, she cried and said she was sorry. She didn't realize how fast she went through the money. How can I build a life with someone who doesn't tell me everything?"

"What would you have done if she had?" Because when Hawk had tried to tell her he blew through their small savings to start a group for alcoholic firefighters, she had thrown the checkbook at him.

"I don't know. Yelled, probably. But maybe I could have stopped her before it was too late."

"Maybe. Can I ask you something else?" She grabbed the pillow Hawk used and pressed it to her face. She inhaled his woodsy scent.

"Since I just told you my biggest secret, I don't see why not."

"Do you love her?"

"What does that have to do with it?"

"Everything. Relationships are about the good and the bad. We have to accept each other, flaws and all. She loves you very much. She told me that. If you can't imagine waking up beside anyone else, or having anyone else beside you when your life turns on its head, then you should rethink your decision."

He didn't say anything.

"Ken, are you still there?"

"Even if I do decide to go through with this, what are we going to do about the storm?"

"We just need the bridge to go down. Even if it's just you two at the hotel, that's all that matters. Will you marry her?"

"I need to think. But thanks, Aria. I appreciate the call. I'll call Celine, and we can talk." He ended the call.

She swapped her sweater for her favorite sweatshirt to give her the courage she would need to explain to Hawk her intentions and ask him to forgive her. Her phone rang again. "Please be Hawk."

Her stomach dropped. Patrick. Holding him off a few

more hours wouldn't change anything. She wasn't going back to him.

He had asked several times why she was holding off on planning their wedding. Now she knew the answer. She let the call go to voicemail and went after the man she wanted to wake up alongside, to hold her when she was afraid of the dark, to share her secrets with.

CHAPTER TEN

Hawk sat at the bar turning the glass of bourbon in his hand. The storm had taken a turn for the worse. The wind rattled all the windows with its powerful gusts. The high tide threatened to bring the ocean right up to the edge of the hotel's property. The snow dropped from the sky like a solid sheet of white. No one was going anywhere tonight even if the bridge was operational. He wished it was. He wanted to be anywhere but the Hotel Horseman.

"Doesn't look like you've touched your drink." An older guy with red cheeks slid onto the bar stool next to him and stuck out his hand. "I'm John. I'm the gardener on these premises."

"Hawk." They shook. "Don't feel much like drinking." He had ordered his drink on the rocks. The ice had melted, but he never took the glass from the bar.

He had called his sponsor, but the call went to voicemail. He wanted to call Aria, but she had never been good when she found him sitting at a bar. Not that he hadn't given her reason to react that way, but he needed someone right now who wouldn't yell at him.

"Do you want some coffee instead? That's what I'm feeling like with this weather. Hey, Jimmy, take this away and bring us two coffees on me." John pushed the whiskey glass halfway down the bar.

The bartender dumped the drink before Hawk could stop him. "That cost me eight bucks."

"I'm thinking that drink would cost you more than that. What's troubling you?"

Only because this guy was old enough to be his father and kind of reminded him of his captain, he would keep his tone in check, but he wasn't in the mood for a meddler. "I don't have any problems except I'm stuck in this hotel."

"There are worse places to be stuck. Are you traveling with your family?"

Jimmy brought the coffees and went back to the far end of the bar to pour more wine for Ethan and Mike. He gave them a quick wave. Mike raised his glass. Ethan offered up a nod.

"I'm alone this trip." That was an understatement. He had thought for a minute he and Aria would have a chance, but nothing had changed for her. She was probably on the phone with her fiancé, making plans for their life. His stomach twisted into a rope.

"Drink up," John said.

The smell of the coffee made his stomach twist more. "Not much gardening this time of year. How do they keep you busy?" He would rather talk about something else than his companion on this trip.

"Doing this or that. Is it a lady?"

"My brother is a lot like you. Makes friends everywhere he goes. Me, I don't like to talk much. So, if you don't mind, I just want to sit here with my thoughts. Thanks for the coffee." He grabbed the cup and slid off the stool.

"Women are tough to figure out. I've been married fifty-five years, and I still can't understand my wife half the time. I do know I'd do whatever it takes to make her keep putting up with me. I'd be lost without her." John kept his gaze on the television behind the bar.

"Sounds like you love her. She's a lucky lady." He glanced around the room for a way to escape. The tables had filled with people talking and laughing. Even most of the seats at the bar were taken. This storm hadn't dampened anyone's mood except his. If he didn't want to go back to the hotel room, he wasn't sure where he could go to get some peace and quiet.

"Are you in a hurry?" John tapped on the bar.

"Not really."

"Then have a seat. Your brother seems like a good man. I like meeting strangers too."

"And giving advice."

"My wife does say sometimes I should mind my own business, but when I see a young man like you staring into a drink with the weight of the world on his shoulders, I figure the good Lord put me in your path for a reason. And that reason might be to buy you a coffee."

He slid back on the stool and poured cream into his coffee. "What advice are you going to give me about my lady?"

"Do you love her?"

"Yup."

"Then what's the problem? Love conquers all. Haven't you heard?"

"She doesn't trust me anymore, and I don't think she ever will." The coffee was as bitter as his attitude at the moment.

John sipped his. "Hmm. You did something to make her question you. How are you going to make it right?"

"If she won't put some faith in me, there isn't anything I can do. She's always going to believe I haven't changed." Just like she believed he was driving in the snowstorm with no destination because he would be reckless enough to do that.

"You in construction or a line of work like that?"

"Firefighter. Why?"

"You're in pretty good shape. A firefighter, huh? That would make you brave, determined, maybe a little fearless."

"I guess. I'm just doing my job. I don't think about any of that stuff."

"A man like you wouldn't give up so easily. You don't quit looking for people in a burning building until everyone is out, do you?" John drank his coffee and put the mug down with a thud.

"We do everything we can to save anyone caught in a fire. I also don't go running into a building without my gear, if you get me. I don't see how this is the same thing. She's made herself pretty clear."

"Jimmy, another round for me and Hawk."

"I'm good with this one, thanks." He had barely touched his. Coffee would keep him up all night, and the only reason he wanted for lack of sleep was Aria beneath him.

"Hawk, you're a sensible man. I can tell just by looking at you. But matters of the heart have nothing to do with sensible. If every time you're with her she feels like home, and every time you're away from her, you're wondering when you'll see her again, that's all that matters. You say you love her. You can't give up on that."

The wash sink behind the bar spurted water from the faucet in every direction. Jimmy jumped back and yelled. John hopped off the stool and ran to help. "Hang on, Jimmy. I've got this one."

The coffee grew cold. He pushed the mug away. He had not given up on Aria, but she gave up on him a long time ago. Coming here with her had been a mistake he'd have to live with. Phoenix would say he told him so. He deserved that. It was time to move on.

A hand gripped his arm. "Hawk?"

His heart picked up speed as Aria stood before him. "What are you doing here?" He moved off the stool. Her touch was too much to handle. He needed to get used to living without it again.

"I came looking for you."

"Is that my old sweatshirt?"

She wore one of his department sweatshirts. He'd forgotten he had that one. The navy had faded, and the collar was ripped in several places. It hung to her knees, and she had rolled the sleeves up, but she looked so good, blood ran to his groin.

She glanced down as if she had forgotten too, then back at him. "Yeah. It's my favorite. I wore it so much, it's falling apart."

He shouldn't think too much about the fact it's his

sweatshirt she wears. "What does your fiancé think about you wearing my clothes?"

"He's never seen it. Can we go somewhere and talk?"

More secrets from this guy. That made him feel pretty good. "Talk about what? You said all you needed to say. I get it. You're through with me."

The lights flickered. Some of the color drained from her face. If they lost power again, he wouldn't leave her alone. But that was it. He'd sleep in his truck tonight, or he'd risk going out again and break into the firehouse for a place to stay.

"I need to talk to you, and it's too loud in here. The brown room is quiet. And there's a fire burning. Please, Hawk."

When she said his name, especially in bed, he wanted to do anything for her. She was the person he wanted to be with more than anyone else. The possibility of being with her again was something that helped him get cleaned up.

He gestured for her to lead the way. She settled on the brown couch by the fire. Only one other couple sat at a table in the corner of the room. The lights flickered again and almost went out. She folded and unfolded her hands in her lap.

He put his hands over hers. "Are you nervous about the lights or talking with me?"

"Both." She let out a deep breath.

"Then let me say something first. Okay?" John's words still swam in his head.

"I'd really like to get this out."

"So would I. Aria, all I want is for you to be happy. I wish it could be with me, but it's not. I don't like it, but

I'll get over it. You should marry your guy and live happily ever after or whatever the hell women say in their romance novels." He was doing the noble thing, but his gut went sour anyway.

"So, that's it then. We have one argument, and you're ready to run. You don't even want to fight for us. You just give up."

"You gave up on us. Well, on me. I deserved that. I didn't give you a reason to stay with me, and now that I want to try again, you still won't try to trust me."

"I know I should do a better job of trusting you, but you scare the hell out of me." She unrolled a sleeve of the shirt and rolled it back up again.

"I guess that just proves my point that you can't be with me. You don't have to say anymore. I understand. You want me gone. As soon as the snow let's up, I'll leave."

"Would you just shut up?"

"What?"

"You heard me. You are someone I could never be. You are spontaneous and fearless. I plan every minute of my day. I have to control everything to the point I choke the life out of it because if I don't, then my anxieties sneak up on me. I'm in my forties and I'm afraid of the dark. Can I be any more pathetic?"

His heart turned to ash for what she and her sisters went through. Anytime she brought it up, he wanted to punch her father's lights out. Lucky for that bastard he was already dead. "You're anything but. You're smart, sophisticated, sexy. I'm the darkness in your life now. Look how great you've done without me. I don't want to spend my life worrying you'll wake up one day and realize getting back with me is the biggest mistake of your life. Take care, Aria."

He couldn't stand there another second because if he did he'd kiss her, and then he'd never want to stop. He could convince her to stay with him. She'd taken off her ring and came here to tell him how she felt, but she deserved better than him. She deserved a life with a man in one piece unlike him who had broken so many times all the pieces couldn't even be found.

The lobby was empty except for Henry behind the desk who waved to him as he made his way to the elevator. He'd pack his things and go. It was best for everyone. The doors slid open and on a long breath, he stepped inside.

"Hawk, wait." Aria jumped into the elevator as the doors closed. "Can you hear me out, please?"

He hit the button for the sixth floor. "There's nothing left to say. I brought this on. I take full responsibility. You don't have anything to worry about. I won't ever mention the past couple of days to anyone." Not that they ran in the same crowds, but he wouldn't even tell his brother who he shared a lot with.

"You aren't the only one with a say. You don't get to decide for me—"

The lights flickered and went out, throwing complete blackness over them. The elevator screeched to a halt.

"I need the light." Panic shook her voice with two fists. "Now, Hawk. I need light now."

"Hang on. Let me get my phone." He patted his pants for his phone and remembered he'd left it in the room when he took off his jeans. He was still wearing his sweatpants.

"I can't breathe. There isn't enough air in here." The slaps of flesh against the walls echoed in the small chamber.

"Aria, I'm right here. You're okay."

"I'm not okay," she yelled.

He reached for her, but he missed. "I need you to stay still."

"I have to keep moving."

He waited for her to make another pass around the elevator and grabbed her. He wrapped his arms around her and held her to his chest. She struggled against his grip, but he kept hold.

"Babe, you're going to be fine." He whispered into her hair.

"Turn on your phone light." She tried to wiggle from him.

"Stop fighting me, Aria."

"Your phone."

"I left it in the room."

She groaned. "I left mine there too."

"Do you want to sing?" That's how he got her to relax in the past. If he could get her to focus on him and sing along to any stupid song he could think of, she would come down out of the panic attack.

"No."

He sang a few lines of their favorite Nat King Cole song. "Come on, babe. You know I can't sing by myself. I'm terrible at it." He tried again.

"You are pretty bad." Her small chuckle egged him on.

"Then help me out."

"Thinks I am..." She stumbled over a few words.

"That's it." He swayed to the melody forcing her to move too.

She started to relax in his embrace and weaved her arms around his waist.

"See, it's going to be fine. I want to use the emergency phone to make sure someone knows we're in here. I have to move away, but only for a second."

"No." She gripped him tighter.

He leaned to the side, but kept one arm around her, and felt for the button panel. His fingers slid over a smooth wall. He was pretty sure a few steps would bring him what he wanted.

"Walk with me." He stepped to the right, and she followed, holding on to his waist for dear life.

"Thank you," she said.

"Don't worry about it." What had she been doing the past two years if she hadn't told the guy she was about to marry about her past?

He found the phone and picked it up, hoping this hotel followed elevator call requirements.

"This is Henry at the front desk. We're aware you're stuck in the elevator located in the lobby."

"Henry, it's Hawk Egan. I'm here with Aria Scirocco. How soon can you get us out? The emergency lights haven't come on."

"I apologize. Something is terribly wrong with the generator. I dispatched a call to the fire department, but the storm is making it hard for them to get here. Please bear with us, sir. I'm on it."

"Thanks, Henry. Keep me posted. Neither of us have a cell phone, and Aria isn't feeling well."

"Yes, sir." Henry hung up.

"Okay, babe, they are on their way." He hoped she'd make it till someone showed up.

Aria's heart raced in her chest. Sweat ran down her back and over her lip. Her hands shook. She was going to have a heart attack right in the elevator and die. She clung to Hawk like a life preserver, but he couldn't really help her. She stood on this island of panic all by herself and wouldn't get off until those doors opened up. She had always been able to manage the attacks as long as the space she was in was larger than a closet. She also carried her phone with her or the small flashlight she hung on her keychain. Even in her home, she kept a flashlight in every room and checked the batteries on a regular basis. Just like Hawk told her to.

"Do you want to sit?" Hawk's voice drifted through her thoughts.

"I guess so." She wished she at least had a match.

He guided her to the side of the elevator, and they took a seat with their backs to the wall. He laced their fingers together and hooked his leg over hers.

She took slow, deep breaths and counted backward from a hundred. Her heart started to slow some.

"Do you want to sing again?" he said.

She rested her head against his shoulder. "I can't believe you remembered the singing."

"I remember everything about us."

Her insides warmed like fondue chocolate. She wished she could explain to Celine and Ken that marriage would be hard. There would be days when someone wouldn't want to see the other, and there would be fights. But when it's true love, any storm could be weathered together.

"Hawk, I'm sorry I wasn't there for you when you needed me most."

"I gave you plenty of reasons to distrust me. Let's talk about something else."

"I'm sorry about panicking. It's so stupid. If I had been here alone, I would have screamed and screamed until my voice broke. I would have probably broke every fingernail trying to pry open the door and climb out. Lucky for me you were here."

"It's not stupid. It happens. Give yourself a break. Besides, if I hadn't stormed off, you wouldn't have followed me."

"You had every right to be mad and walk away."

"Sometimes it's easier for me to walk away than to engage. If I can give myself a chance to breathe, I'm not as likely to want to drink. Staying sober was important for me to prove to you I was worth a chance."

"We're a bit of a mess, you and I."

He laughed and put an arm around her. "I guess so."

"Maybe that's why we keep coming back to each other." She kept returning to him because he understood her in ways no one else ever had. He had his own demons and never judged her for hers. The rush of adrenaline seeped from her body. Fatigue took its place. She snuggled closer to him.

"Staying together because we're both dysfunctional isn't a good reason," he said.

Her heart ached. She had let him down. "I don't want to be the person who brings out the worst in you."

more. He gripped her bottom and pulled her down further. Her head dropped back on her neck, and she called out his name.

The emotional roller coaster she'd been on all day added to the rise and fall of her orgasm as it shook her body. A tear slid down her face, but that was from the rush and not from sadness. He dug his fingers into her bottom and nipped the side of her neck as he came too.

He rested his forehead on her chest. "I love you, Aria."

CHAPTER ELEVEN

The elevators opened, and Aria hurried into the lobby. The open space expanded her lungs. Henry waited for them with bottled water and a big smile.

"Are you two all right?" He handed a bottle to her.

"We're great." Hawk caught her eye and winked.

Heat bloomed on her cheeks. She was certain Henry knew what they were doing in his elevator. And even if Henry didn't, just thinking about being with Hawk sent delicious warmth over her skin.

"The power seems to be back on, and the good news, there is a break in the storm." Henry clapped his hands.

"Hey, babe?"

She turned to him. "Yeah?"

"I have an idea."

"What's that?"

"Trust me."

"Hawk, tell me."

"Let's get our coats and go for a walk. I think it would be good for us, and I want to show you the firehouse." His smile was wide and bright. She couldn't tell him no.

The path had been shoveled some and made walking easier. Hawk laced his fingers through hers, and smiled down at her with ease. She never tired of walking with him like this.

She loved the way he carried himself with his wide shoulders held back and his chin up. For all that he had been through, he looked everyone in the eye. He wasn't ashamed of his mistakes.

They walked along Beach Street. The ocean was dark and angry as its white caps crashed on the sand over and over as if to punish someone or something for getting in its way. The wind blew in from the east and snuck under her coat to cover her in a cold chill. "The snow might've stopped, but that wind is ferocious."

"Are you cold?" Hawk said.

"Uh, yeah. It's freezing out, but it's okay because I'm with you."

"Babe, you're making me a happy man." He tugged her close and planted a kiss on her lips.

"After what we just did in the elevator, you made me pretty happy too."

They crossed Decatur Street. They were the only two outside. Not many people lived on the island in the off season. A hush fell over the town. The snow covered the noises around them like a blanket.

"You know, um, there's something that occurred to me about what we've been doing."

"No condom," she said.

He let out a long breath. "Yeah. That. I want you to know I'm clean. You don't have to worry."

"I wasn't." She was a little concerned about getting pregnant, but she'd worry about that if later, if she had even had to. "You don't have to worry either."

"Does that mean you and your fiancé haven't had sex yet?"

She pressed her lips together. Patrick would never have sex without a condom. Even during that short time when she was on the pill, he wouldn't risk it. "Leave it at you don't have anything to worry about."

"You can't blame a guy for hoping." He wrapped his arm around her and pulled her close.

"Do you ever think about being a dad?" They continued their walk down Beach Street.

"Sometimes, but I don't know if it's for me. I didn't have the best role model."

She swallowed the disappointment in her throat. If they had made a baby, what would he say? "I didn't either, but I wonder if I could do a better job than my father did."

"You'd make a great mom."

She blinked away the tears wanting to spill. They walked in silence for a while. She allowed the image of them starting a family to form, but she didn't want to dream too much.

Hawk stopped in front of an old Victorian painted yellow. Some of the shutters hung crooked on their hinges. The front post of the railings were rotted and in need of paint. Pieces of the broken walkway poked out from under the snow.

"There was a fire there."

"How can you tell?"

"Come see."

The side of the house had streaks of black against the wood slats. She had missed that as they were passing by. He led her around the back, and she gasped.

The back of the house was covered in black soot. The wall had a gaping hole in it like an old man missing his front teeth.

Hawk continued around the back. The snow was deep enough to get inside her ankle-length boots and wet her socks. The other side of the house held the most damage. The windows had been blown away. The soot was thicker and darker. It was almost impossible to tell the house was even yellow from this side.

Through the window, the beams hung like pendulums from the ceiling.

"The fire started here," he said.

"I hope no one was hurt."

"Me too."

She didn't have to ask to know he was thinking about Wyatt. The crease between his brow had returned, and the sadness in his eyes told her everything. She squeezed his hand. She hadn't been there for him then. She could try and be there for him now.

"Was it hard for you to go back to work after?" She hadn't asked him that before. She'd stayed away, wallowing in her own self-pity. She had hurt for him and for Wyatt, but she didn't know how to support him.

He shoved his hands in his pockets and looked down the street. "It's still hard. I miss him. He was my big brother."

"Hawk, I'm so sorry you lost him. I know that's not much, and it's too late, but I am."

"I just wish I hadn't been such a jerk that day. If I

hadn't been fucking up like usual, he might still be here." He sniffled, but that could have just as easily been from the cold and the wind.

"Wyatt wouldn't blame you."

"Doesn't matter if he would. I do, and that's plenty. I want to take a look inside."

"Seriously? Isn't that dangerous?"

"Just step where I step. I love these old houses. This one might be able to be saved." He climbed the back, cement steps.

"You would live here?" She grabbed onto the back of his coat to keep from getting too far away from him.

"On the island? Sure. It's not far from the department. It's quiet in the winter. I need that. It's big enough for a family." He stopped inside the kitchen and looked around. "Would you live here?"

The kitchen was small but well laid out. The cabinets were wood, and with some sandpaper and paint, they'd be good as new. She didn't have a lot of money, but together they could probably fix it up. She was getting ahead of herself, pretending, and that could be dangerous.

"I never thought about it, but I think so. I could probably get a lot of clients just from the Hotel Horseman. It's not far from some of the bigger cities. It might be nice, except for the broken windows."

He laughed. "Yeah, those should be fixed first." He moved into the dining room, testing the floor with his toe each time.

A large crystal chandelier hung from the center of the ceiling. It swayed from the breeze coming in from those broken windows. The crystals were covered in soot.

They would probably catch the morning sunlight coming in off the ocean on a bright day.

"I talked with Mack earlier."

"Did she sing my praises?" Sarcasm dripped from his lips.

"She's worried about me. She doesn't want to see me hurt. I think it's because she's going through a rough divorce right now. Her ex is a real piece of work, like our dad."

"And like me?"

"No, Hawk. Nothing like you. I wanted you to know my sisters might not be on board with us getting together. I don't want things to be hard on you."

He gripped her shoulders and held her gaze. His light-brown eyes shone in the murky room. "I don't give a damn what they say. If you want me, then the rest of the world can go to hell."

"I was thinking the same thing."

He kissed her long and hard. Heat pooled between her legs. Suddenly, the cold didn't bother her. She was ready to go back to the hotel.

"Good." He wrapped his arms around her waist and pulled her close. "This thing between us feels right again. Like it was in the beginning."

The feelings she had for him knocked her off balance. "You see me in a way no one else does."

"That's good for me, right?" The mischievous smile was on his face.

"You're kind of hard to resist when you look at me like that."

"Then let's finish this tour and go back to the hotel so I can get lucky." He wagged his eyebrows.

She swatted at him, but the effervescence of joy expanded in her chest. "Are you supposed to be in here after a fire?"

"Nope, but that doesn't stop me. Houses tell stories, and that includes the fires that ravaged them. Like, if this were arson, the fire in here would tell us that. Or if it were a Christmas tree that caught fire, we'd know that too." He gripped her arm as she tried to pass him.

"What's the matter?"

"There's a hole under the rug."

A hole stuck out from the side of the area rug. She hadn't noticed it and would've fallen in. "Why didn't the rug turn to ashes?"

"It's probably made of a non-flammable material."

"Can we get out of here now? This place might've been beautiful once, but she's sad now, maybe even a little angry because of what happened to her. I wouldn't want to be here alone in the dark."

CHAPTER TWELVE

She and Hawk had dinner in their room. She had checked her phone as soon as they returned. Patrick had called twice. His messages were more frantic. She was going to need to deal with him soon but not now. Now, she and Hawk sat up in bed on top of the covers. Their lovemaking earlier and the long walk in the cold had them both spent. They just wanted to be with each other. She didn't care what they were doing, as long as they kept doing it together. The television was on the weather station, but the sound was muted.

Fear had her avoiding Patrick. He wasn't going to take the news well, not that he should. She debated telling him in person when she returned home. The breakup might come better if they were face to face. She should have thought of that before she called the first time.

Her phone vibrated with a text message. Hawk raised an eyebrow in question. He must be wondering when she was going to tell Patrick about them.

"It's Celine."

Did you hear? The bridge is down.

Great news. Ken?

She had been so wrapped up in her own drama, she had neglected her bride's needs. That wasn't like her, but neither was throwing caution to the wind.

He says he's coming. Thank you.

Looked like two couples would end up happy this weekend. She wished she wouldn't be hurting Patrick, but it was too late to change that. She had been selfish. Or crazy, but for once she didn't care.

She ran her fingers through Hawk's hair. "I love your hair longer. Don't cut it."

"I can't let it get too long. Hair is flammable. What did Celine want?"

She sat up. "Oh, the bridge is down. Looks like there's going to be a wedding after all. I have so much to do. This little vacation has had some great moments, but now I have to get back to work."

"If the bridge is down, and you're going to be working, would you mind if I went to Virginia after all?"

"Virginia? Is that where you were headed? I thought you heard my license plate on the scanner." A quick worry he wasn't telling the truth passed through her thoughts, but she shoved it away. The knee-jerk reaction would take a little while to disappear. They had suffered a lot together, but she'd get there.

"I heard your license plate and came running. I was at the firehouse before I left. I was on my way to meet Phoenix."

"A boys' trip?"

He leaned his head against the back of the bed and closed his eyes. "Promise me you won't laugh."

"Why would I laugh?" She shifted to get a better look at him and tried to read the vacant expression on his face.

"Phoenix and I started a retreat for firefighters dealing with grief. We are holding it in Virginia at the Cavalier Hotel this year."

"Why would I laugh at that?"

"It's kind of sappy." He opened one eye and gave her a quizzical look.

She placed a hand on his face. "It's wonderful. Wyatt would be proud of you. It's what you wanted to do years ago."

"It was the wrong time then. I was still a mess. You were right to tell me I was out of my mind. I couldn't pay the light bill; how could I handle something the size of this?"

"I have been horrible to you." She flopped back on the bed and stared at the ceiling. "Are you certain you want to start over with me?"

"There's something you should know."

"That sounds ominous." She turned to face him.

"I told Phoenix I was here with you. He doesn't think we should be together any more than your sister does. I guess I should've told you sooner."

"Both of our families are against us? I want to throw reason away, but what if they're right? I didn't support you. I didn't honor our vows either. You could wake up one day and decide you don't want to be with me any longer."

He was so worried it would be she that left, but she

had as much to worry about. He could find someone who would never judge him, and what if she ended up judging him again? Had she changed at all? Had she learned to be different since the divorce?

"Let's put the past behind us. I want to move on. It's how I'm managed to deal with all my anger and my drinking. I don't want to rehash our past, okay? We'll promise to start from here."

"I could do that. I want to do that, but I hope our siblings will learn to respect our choices and accept us."

"They'll come around. Even Mack."

"Yeah, even my bullheaded sister, I hope. Go to Virginia. How long is the retreat?"

"It's a week. I'd have a few days there."

"Then go."

"What if the power goes out again while you're here? This place doesn't seem to have the best electricity."

"I'll keep your flashlight with me the whole time, and I'll stay out of the elevator. You should go. I insist." She would get this relationship right this time and prove Mack and Phoenix wrong.

"Thanks, babe." He jumped off the bed with a wide smile. "I'm going to stretch my legs a little and call Phoenix. I'll leave first thing in the morning."

She needed to call Patrick back anyway. That conversation should be between her and him. He deserved to at least have his privacy respected. Hawk closed the door behind him. She turned on every light in the room and checked the flashlight. Of course it still worked; it was Hawk's.

They hadn't talked about what they would do once they got home. He'd leave in the morning and not be back until mid-week. She'd be back Sunday afternoon. She would take a page from his book and just go with it. She didn't have to plan every step. Things would work out. They were working out now. He wasn't going anywhere. She could trust him.

She dialed Patrick's number and held her breath, but the call went to voicemail. He couldn't be too concerned about what she wanted to say if he wasn't answering the phone every time she called. Once or even twice she could understand, but her calls were adding up. She left a message and said to call her in the morning.

She didn't want to talk to him tonight. Tonight she wanted to spend every second in Hawk's arms before he left. Tonight would have to hold her over until his return. He was like a drug, and she couldn't get enough.

Hawk blinked his eyes open. Was that banging on the door, or was he dreaming? The room was still dark except for the light spilling in from the half-shut bathroom door. After the elevator, Aria wanted a light on when they went to bed. She lay on her side facing away from him. Her back rose and fell in a slow rhythm. Someone banged on the door again. Definitely not a dream.

He grabbed his underwear and pulled it on. He looked out the peephole. Some guy fidgeted outside the door. Whoever he was, he faced down the hall, offering only his profile. Hawk couldn't see his face. He left the chain on but opened the door.

"We're sleeping here. What's with the banging?"

Sleep splintered his voice into fragments. He blinked against the light in the hall.

The man's face went slack. "What are you doing here?"

"That's my question. You must have the wrong room." He started to shut the door, but the man stopped him.

"You're Hawk. Where's Aria? Is she here? Aria? Oh shit, you're not dressed." Patrick tried to see over his shoulder, but he had this guy by three or four inches.

Probably should have put some pants on. Aria hadn't spoken to her fiancé about the change in their status. He kind of felt bad for the guy. "Hang on, okay. You're making a racket. Let me get some pants on, and we can talk."

"Hawk?" Aria's voice slid through the opening in the door. The color drained from Patrick's face.

Hawk hung his head and eased his grip on the door putting slack on the chain. "It's for you."

She stumbled from the bed and yanked on clothes. Patrick kicked the door, and it hit his shoulder knocking him off balance. Fury burned in his veins. He slammed the door shut, wrenched off the chain, and tugged the door back open. He grabbed Patrick by the collar of his fancy dress shirt and dragged him into the room.

"You ever do that again, and I'll knock you out."

"Hawk." Aria's voice held a warning.

She had managed to throw on his sweatshirt and his sweatpants. He wanted to laugh at her choice of clothes. Was that a conscious decision or something Freud would have a field day with? "He needs to keep his shit together and not hit people with doors."

"What's going on here?" Patrick's gaze bounced between the two of them.

Like he had to spell it out. He grabbed his jeans and his phone, then shoved his feet into his boots. "I'll be downstairs if you need me."

"Oh no, you're not going anywhere." Patrick swayed on his feet and pointed a finger at Aria. "I can't believe you would cheat on me with him." Each word slurred over the other.

"Are you drunk?" he said.

"So what if I am? I've been calling my fiancé for days only to find out from her sister she's here with you. She told me to leave Aria alone, but I would do no such thing."

For once, he wanted to hug Mack and her big mouth.

"I'm sorry. This isn't how I wanted you to find out. I was trying to reach you," Aria said.

"Is that what your calls were going to be about? You're having sex with your ex-husband?" Patrick grabbed the wall and shook his head.

"You should go. I don't want you talking to her when you're drunk." That would be the last warning he'd give. If her fiancé didn't walk away on his own steam, he'd escort him to the door.

"I wanted to tell you we're not right for each other. I don't want to marry you." Aria tilted her chin up.

"When did you decide that? When he tricked you into getting into bed with him?"

"I'd decided a long time ago. It's just been this weekend that I realized I'd been putting off the inevitable. I am sorry. You shouldn't have found out this way."

"I don't need to be here for this." He really wanted to get the hell out.

"Don't fucking move. I'm not through with you." Patrick pointed a finger at him now.

"Pat, you'd better put that finger away."

"Patrick. And don't fucking tell me what to do when you've been fucking my wife." Spit flew from his mouth.

He stood his full height and squared his shoulders. "She's not your wife. I felt bad about the way things went down here, but I'm not sorry. She belongs with me."

"How could you sleep with him? He's trash." Pat ignored his last comment and turned his attention back to Aria.

"Stop saying nasty things. That's not necessary. I know you're upset, and you have every right to be—"

"You're damn right I have the right to be pissed off. You betrayed me. You lied to me. Did you have this whole thing planned?"

"No, of course not."

"You disgust me. You're a whore just like your cheating father." Pat shoved Aria. She stumbled over the edge of the bed and fell.

His vision blurred. All the rage he kept caged up burst out. He hauled off and punched Pat right in the jaw. His head snapped back, and he crumpled to the floor. Hawk grabbed him by the collar and yanked him up.

"Get out." He opened the door and dumped Pat in the hallway.

"Hawk, my God. You hit him. You promised you wouldn't fight."

He shook out his hand. "I promised I wouldn't get into a bar fight. This doesn't count. That bastard put his hands on you."

"I appreciate what you're trying to do, but this is my battle to fight, not yours," she said.

"I want to protect you."

"You can't, and I don't need you to. Not this time. I know I'm a mess when the lights go out, but this isn't the same thing. And if I'm ever really going to get better, I need to face this myself. Alone."

"Babe, the things he said to you. I can't let him get away with that."

"I can handle him. Not to mention, he's drunk. I can't let him get back in a car. I'm going to get him some coffee."

"Babe, please let me deal with him." He didn't want her to go away mad. He wasn't sorry he hit Pat. He'd do it again. He might've promised to be better, but he was still him, and no one would disrespect his woman the way that shithead did.

She poked him in the chest. "You stay here until I get back. I can't worry about you while I'm dealing with him."

"At least take your phone." He handed it to her. He wanted her to have a way to reach him if Pat became too much to handle.

She grabbed it and closed the door on him. He was too hotheaded for her. It would end up biting him in the ass someday. He wasn't sorry he punched Pat. He'd do it again.

He didn't trust Pat to behave himself, and every fiber

in his body wanted to protect Aria. She'd been through enough with men who bullied her.

But he understood why she wouldn't want him to fight. She had nursed him back from a few brawls that should have landed him in the hospital. Had that punch to Patrick's face made her second guess her feelings for him?

He wouldn't lose her, especially not to Pat. Pat's money and stability were no match for his love for Aria.

Hopefully, she could see that.

Or he'd be heartbroken.

And that would lead to something far worse.

CHAPTER THIRTEEN

Aria faced Patrick on the sofa in the lobby, but kept a good distance from him. The fireplace sat quiet and dark, making the high-ceilinged room drafty. The snow had not returned, but the wind continued to howl. A chill crept into her bones. She wanted Hawk's arms around her for warmth, but she was still seething from his hitting Patrick. He had promised no more fights, and he did anyway. Patrick should never have done what he did, but hitting him wasn't the answer.

Patrick's lip swelled, and blood had dripped on his white shirt. He sat there with a pout on his face. She had thought him very attractive until recently. She liked his clean-cut look compared to Hawk's rugged jeans and scruffy beard. Patrick never smelled like smoke when he came home, didn't have soot under his fingernails, but looking at him now, Patrick was an ugly person with a cold heart. That's why, deep down, she'd never told him about her father and the things he'd done to her and her sisters.

"Aria, how could you do this to us?"

"It just happened. I didn't plan on it." But she was glad it had happened. Being with Hawk showed her she wasn't right with Patrick.

"Okay, okay. Please come home with me. We can forget this ever happened. I can't live without you." Patrick's words still slurred.

"You're going to have to. Let's get you some coffee." She stood, hoping he'd follow.

"No. I don't need coffee. I need you, and you need me. We're a team. You said so yourself."

"I was wrong. I'm sorry. It's over."

"You're so gullible. Your ex must've brainwashed you. Come home with me tonight."

Anger locked her jaw. She forced a long breath through her nose. "I'm not leaving the hotel. I have a wedding tomorrow."

"Planning weddings isn't a real job. It's time to rethink this business idea. I can help you get a position in my company with stability and growth."

"You sound just like my father." She had been blinded by Patrick's success and the fact he was responsible, and even in those moments when he was sweet to her. But that had been her father too.

"I have a job I love very much, and I'm good at it. I'm sorry I slept with Hawk before telling you we were over, but I'm not sorry I did it, and I don't like you implying I can't think for myself."

"Well, you can't. I mean, my wife wouldn't have to. I can take care of you the way you need to be taken care of."

Her stomach soured. She wanted to hit him herself.

"You need to go. There isn't anything left to say." The engagement ring was upstairs in her luggage still. She should give it back to him. "Why don't you wait here, and I'll go get your ring."

He gripped her arm. His fingers dug into her skin. "Don't go."

"You're hurting me."

His eyes, usually a sky blue, turned black. Her breath caught. A cold dread ran over her body. No one was in the lobby or the brown room. At this late hour, and with the weather, everyone would be in their hotel rooms. Her phone stuck out between the cushion of the sofa and the wicker, out of reach.

"I said don't go. We haven't finished talking." His stale breath made her stomach turn.

She tried to pry his fingers from her arm, but he had a vise grip. "Let go of me."

"You're mine. Not his."

"You don't own me." Her heart picked up speed.

He yanked her and closed the gap between them. Red lines ran through the whites of his eyes. "I won't allow you to go back to that blue-collar firefighter. What will people say when they find out you left me for him?"

"I don't care what people say. I love Hawk." She tilted her chin and tugged her arm to get away.

Patrick slapped her. Her head snapped back, and her tongue got caught between her teeth. The metallic taste of blood coated the inside of her mouth. She kicked his shin and he released her. She ran.

The lights went out.

∾

For a second, Aria lost her sense of direction. The stairs had been in front of her, and that's where she was headed. Her eyes adjusted to the glow from the snow-covered surfaces outside, and somehow she was closer to the elevators. She ran for the brown room. Patrick was fast on her heels.

The brown room didn't have the same kind of windows as the lobby. The room was darker. Her heart clamored around in her chest, and her breathing shallowed. Her head spun. She needed to get to light.

She forced her feet forward when all she wanted to do was cower in a corner until the power came back on. A door to the outside waited right through the brown room. She shoved on the metal push bar, but the door didn't budge. She tried again. The snow must've drifted against it, blocking the way out.

She ran for the ballroom and collided with a round, dinner table. A pain shot up her hip. The room was dark here too because the shutters had been pulled closed against the tall windows. Only small slats of gray light seeped through but did nothing to help her. The panic gripped her throat. Air wouldn't come in or out. She tried to think so the panic would back off, but Patrick's voice calling for her wasn't too far behind. Her only advantage was she knew the hotel better than he did.

Her eyes adjusted again. The room had been set up for the wedding. That meant twenty-five tables large enough for ten people filled the whole room. She weaved around the chairs, hoping the way out was on the other side.

"Aria, come back here." Patrick stood in the doorway. She could make out his white shirt in the darkness.

"Stay away from me." She backed toward the other set of doors that should lead to the kitchen.

"You're being unreasonable. I just want to talk. I know I can convince you to stay with me. Your ex doesn't have anything on me otherwise you wouldn't have left him." He took another step forward with his hands raised.

She had left Hawk because she was scared, and he was behaving much like her father. But the only similarities were the job and the drinking. He would never have cheated on her if she hadn't abandoned him the night Wyatt died. That was on her. Hawk was sweet and kind. He accepted her for who she was. He protected her secrets. "I don't love you, Patrick. Please go and we can forget about this."

"I can't leave here without you." He moved closer.

"Don't take another step. I mean it."

"Or what?" He laughed at her.

The tables had also been set for the big day. The only thing missing was the tall vase centerpieces, but in front of most place settings were the stemless, rose-colored wine glasses she'd brought with her. She threw one at Patrick. It bounced off the table near him and shattered on the floor. She threw another and another, hitting him in the head. It was the break she needed. She ran through the last set of double doors, into the kitchen, and outside into a snowbank.

CHAPTER FOURTEEN

The lights went out, and Hawk cursed. He had to get to Aria in the lobby. How could he have let her go with that piece of shit? She'd be panicking, and Pat wouldn't know how to help her. The elevator was out of the question. He'd take the stairs and run down six flights of steps. Without a light. He'd left his phone in the room. There wasn't time to go back. She needed him even if she decided after all she didn't want him.

He held the railing so he didn't land on his head at the bottom, but without more than a little glow from the snow outside coming through a window, he couldn't see the steps and where the landing on each floor was. This would slow him down, and it pissed him off. At least the building wasn't on fire, and he wasn't running out of air in his tank.

The lobby was empty by the time he got there. He kicked a rocking chair, and it fell over. Where the hell did they go?

"Everything all right in here?" John, the gardener,

wandered into the lobby wearing his pajamas and a blue robe. He held a lantern to light the way.

"I have never been so glad to see anyone. I need your help."

"Then I guess it's a good thing I couldn't sleep. What can I do to help you?"

"Aria is missing. She might be in trouble. I have to find her." If anything happened to her because of that scumbag, he would never be able to live with himself.

"From the look on your face, I say times a ticking. Let's go. I'll be the light."

The snow came up to her knees. Picking each leg up and moving forward was like lifting rocks. Wearing Hawk's sweatpants was a mistake. They were heavy with wet snow and making it harder to move. But she had to keep going. Patrick would find his way out here. She couldn't be sure if she did any damage with that wine glass.

She followed the back path to the parking lot and stopped behind a dumpster to catch her breath. The ocean's waves crashed against the sand only yards away. Their roar and the cries of the wind made it hard to hear if anyone was coming. She wasn't sure where to go, but she had to keep moving. She could bang on someone's door. People stayed on the island all year. She would eventually stumble upon an occupied residence. She hoped. She'd call Hawk to come get her, if he still wanted to after what happened in the room.

"Aria, where are you? I saw you come this way. Please, come back so we can talk. We're going to freeze to death out here." Patrick almost sounded believable, and to anyone who didn't know him, he would. They would say she was the crazy one. Only she knew better. She had to keep moving.

The snow wasn't as high in the street. She could go faster, but she slipped on ice and landed on her back. The fall knocked the wind out of her.

"Aria, I see you. Stop running," Patrick said into the wind.

She rolled to her side and pushed off the ground. Patrick came through the parking lot and under the one lit streetlight. She ran in the opposite direction. The houses were completely dark. She didn't want to waste time running up porches and knocking only to find no one was home. Patrick would be on her in a flash, and there was no telling what he would do. She never believed he'd be violent, but then he never slapped her before either. Now he chased her like a monster in a horror movie.

This was the way she and Hawk had walked earlier. She had thought they were ridiculous out in the snow, but now she was grateful yet again for his spontaneous ways. The burned out house was up ahead. She could get inside and hide. Or die from a panic attack that was bound to happen because she wouldn't be able to see in there.

She risked a glance over her shoulder. Patrick was only a block away. He'd be able to see where she went, but she had to try. She was out of options and frozen to the bone. If she didn't die from a panic attack, she'd die from hypothermia.

She ran around the back of the house. Her footprints

in the snow would give her away. She'd have to rely on a good hiding spot and pretend to be brave.

She climbed up the back steps and into the gaping hole where the door once was. It was darker inside without the glow from the snow, and her eyes needed to adjust again. The fire had been contained to mainly the front room on the first floor, but the smell of smoke still hung heavy in the air. She could almost hear the screams of the residents as they tried to escape.

She needed a place to hide. Her stomach twisted into knots at the prospects. She couldn't go in a closet; that would never work. She eased her way through the kitchen, unsure if the flooring would hold. She couldn't remember the spots Hawk used to step on.

The wind whipped through the broken windows and walls. On the other side of the kitchen was the dining room and then the foyer. The dining room table was set as if a party of guests was about to walk into the room. There was no place in here to hide.

The foyer hosted two coat closets. Her hands shook as she pulled on the first door. The knob came off in her hand.

"Aria, are you here?" Patrick's voice glued her to her spot.

Her heart pounded in her ears. He must be able to hear it too. Should she run upstairs?

"Aria, I saw you come in here. You need to come out now. Really, darling, we can work this out. Let's go back to the hotel and warm up."

Her father would play hide and seek with her. That's what he called it sometimes, knowing she'd hide in the closet, and he could lock the door. When she got a little older, he'd drag her into the closet by her hair.

Hiding in the closet was out. She stepped into the living room, the room ravaged by the fire. She avoided the rug that covered the hole and waited by the broken window. She had no choice now, but to confront Patrick.

Her teeth chattered from either the cold or from fear. She couldn't tell the difference any longer. She thought of Hawk and his smile. The way his hair felt between her fingers. His tenderness when they made love. She wanted those to be the last things she remembered if this ended badly for her.

"Finally." Patrick appeared in the entryway. His chest heaved from following her in such bad conditions.

"This is your last chance to turn around and leave. Hawk is going to come looking for me." She only hoped that were true. He might be halfway to Virginia by now, tired of putting up with her.

"I'm sick of your childish behavior. I've held my tongue with you because of your divorce, and sometimes you seem very skittish at odd moments, but enough is enough. I expect you to behave the way my wife would behave."

"I'm not your wife. I'm not going to be your wife."

"You don't know what you're saying. I've decided I've waited too long for you to set a date. When we get home, we'll make arrangements to be married. We can have a nice reception in the spring. You can even plan it, if you'd like."

"Did you always talk to me like this?"

She couldn't make out his features, but his head

shook. "Of course, I did. How else would I talk to you? Let's go."

"No."

"If you don't come with me now, you will be very sorry. I promise you that." He hissed like a cobra.

She backed against the windowsill.

"Now, Aria. I have had enough of your goddamn foolish behavior. You are acting like a child, and I am going to start treating you like one."

"What is that supposed to mean?" Fear shook her voice, and she hated it.

"If you push me, I will show you. If you come with me quietly, I will forget all about this stunt of yours and your infidelity. And we are going to have sex with the lights out like normal people do. You're going to allow me to touch you the way I want, and you're going to like it. Are we clear?"

"Fuck you, Patrick."

He lunged for her.

"Wait, don't move. The floor —" But it was too late.

Patrick landed on the center of the area rug. He and the carpet slipped through the hole that went to the basement. He crashed and banged and screamed the whole way down.

"Aria, please help. I'm hurt. My back. My legs. I'm so sorry for what I said. I didn't mean any of it. I was mad because you cheated on me, but I forgive you. I truly do. Please, Aria, help me. Call for help." Patrick cried through his words.

She should feel something, but her insides were as frozen as her skin. She had been blind and foolish. She got involved with this man because on paper he looked good, but that wasn't what was important. Inside, he was sick. He was the man more like her father than Hawk ever was.

"Aria, do you hear me, goddamn it? I need an ambulance."

The tears ran down her cheeks. Her legs gave up and she slid to the floor. Her wet clothes stuck to her. Her muscles ached. She only wanted to rest, but not in here. She climbed through the broken window, as Patrick continued to yell, and slid down the snow drift. She would get help. In a minute.

CHAPTER FIFTEEN

John drove up and down every street in town while Hawk pointed the light on houses, between stores, and along the beach. There was no sign of Aria or Pat. He had followed their footprints out the back of the hotel, but they ended on the street where the snowplow had come through.

"I'll circle around one more time." John signaled left and eased the truck around the turn.

"I hope he didn't take her off the island."

"We'll find her. She's here somewhere. I can feel it. Try her phone again."

John had lent him his phone. He'd called Aria a dozen times, but she hadn't answered. He dialed again, but again the same result. "How can you be so sure she's still in town?"

"Do you believe she would have left without saying goodbye to you? I only spent a little time with her, but she didn't strike me that way. She's also working that wedding tomorrow. I don't believe she would let her client down." John made another turn down a tight street.

"You're right. She would never walk away from this wedding even if she would walk away from me."

John raised an eyebrow. "Don't go letting doubt cloud your thoughts. She loves you, and you love her, and you'll work it all out once we find her."

"Do you have kids?" John seemed like the kind of man he would've liked as a father. His own father never offered encouragement.

"I have four daughters." John sat up straighter in the seat. His smile was as bright as the headlights on this dark night.

"They're lucky to have you. You give good advice."

"What about you, son? Are you close with your father?"

"No, sir." He'd spare John all the gory details.

"I'm sorry to hear that. Might be time to start a family of your own and break the chain."

He wished he did have a family of his own so he could be a better father than his was. His breath caught. He and Aria hadn't been using a condom. Could they have…

"I do declare." John stopped the truck and pointed out the window.

The truck's headlights spotlighted a person sitting against the side of the burned out house. Her legs were drawn up, and her head rested on her knees.

Hawk jumped from the seat and ran through the snow. He should have thought about this house, but he never imagined she would come here.

His heart raced to pump air through his lungs. He

thought he heard someone yelling. He squatted beside her. She didn't move.

"Aria? You're okay now. I'm here."

Aria heard her name from somewhere far away. Patrick must still be calling for help. She needed to get an ambulance, but she couldn't move.

A hand was placed on her head. She looked up and blinked. A bright, white light broke open the darkness. The silhouette of a man hunkered down. She let out a long breath.

"You came for me."

Hawk gathered her in his arms. "I was worried."

"Thank you." She settled against his warmth and inhaled his familiar scent.

"Aria, if you want to stay with Patrick, or be by yourself, I understand. I'm not going to stop you. I just want you to be safe and happy."

She gripped him tighter, never wanting to let him go again. "I love you, Hawk."

"You do? In the elevator, you didn't say anything after I did. And then when I hit what's his name in the room…"

"I was mad that you hit Patrick, but that doesn't change my feelings for you. I'm not leaving again."

He kissed the top of her head. "You leaving me was the best thing you could have done for me. It's what I needed to get my act together. I only wanted a chance to prove to you I was different. Let's get out of here."

She slid her cold hand into his warm one, and he pulled her up. "We need an ambulance."

"Are you hurt?"

"Not me. Patrick. He fell in that hole." She pointed over her shoulder. "He came after me. I'm pretty sure he was going to hurt me. I tried to stop him, but he was too angry to hear."

John ran toward them with a blanket. "Wrap this around your shoulders. I called for backup when you didn't come right over. I thought maybe you broke something. Is that someone yelling?"

"Looks like we have an injury." Hawk shook his head.

"Get her inside the truck to warm up. I'll stay here with the injured party."

"Did you come with a firetruck?" She realized the lights were so bright they couldn't be coming from a pickup.

John laughed.

"We sure did. John is a member of the volunteer department. He offered to help. I'm eternally grateful."

Hawk helped her into the truck and turned up the heat pointing the vents in her direction. "You need to get out of those wet clothes."

"That's not one of your smoother lines." The truck's heat made her fingers tingle.

"I'm serious. You're soaked. Can you do it, or do you need me to help you?" He yanked off his sweatshirt.

"Hawk?"

"Yeah?" He held the shirt to her. "Take this."

She swapped her wet shirt for his dry one. "While I

was sitting in the snow, trying to catch my breath, I thought about…." She wasn't sure how to go on.

"What about?"

"What would you say if we made a baby?" She held her breath.

He gripped her hands. "Is that possible?"

"Are you calling me old?"

"No way. It's just…I mean…I don't know what I mean except if you're pregnant I just got made the luckiest man in the world." He gathered her in his arms. "Shit, Aria, I was just thinking about how much I wanted a family with you. You are making all my dreams come true."

"Don't get too excited yet. It's only a possibility. We won't know for a while."

"If we didn't this time, we'll keep trying."

"I like the sound of that." Her love for this man warmed her insides. She would never be cold with him in her life.

"Get out of those wet pants too. Come on. I'll block anyone from seeing." He waved his fingers in a give-me gesture. His mischievous grin tugged on his lips.

She wiggled out of the sweatpants. Her legs were cold and red. "Are you going to give me your pants too?"

He wrapped the blanket around her legs. "I'll give you anything you want, but tonight I want to get you warm, take you back to that hotel, and hold you."

"That sounds like the best idea I've heard in a long time."

"I can help you tomorrow at the wedding if you want."

She placed a hand on his beard-covered cheek. "I

want you to go help Phoenix. I have the rest of my life to have you by my side. When we get home, I want to start over."

"You mean that?"

"With every fiber in my body. I love you, Hawk Egan. I want to spend the rest of my life with you the way we always planned."

"I won't let you down this time."

"You couldn't possibly. You are the light that guides me."

BUT THERE'S MORE...

Dear Reader,

Thank you for reading No More Darkness. I hope you enjoyed it as much as I enjoyed writing Aria and Hawk's story.

Turn the page for a sneak peek at chapter one in the next book in the series—Through the Darkness. *The only way to find the truth is to fight back.*

Please consider leaving an honest review. Reviews help authors.

THROUGH THE DARKNESS - CHAPTER ONE

Phoenix Egan should've sent a mayday call sooner. Standing inside a burning building wasn't the same as fighting a fire in the movies. No real firefighter would be able to see where he or she was going. He had trained hundreds of times for this moment, but his heart still took off like a Jet Ski. His oxygen tank would deplete faster if he didn't calm down, and then he'd really be screwed.

He couldn't see a thing. Blackness met him at every turn. The kind of darkness that swallowed up whatever was around and made it disappear forever. His oxygen tank beeped with the deafening alert of running out. Running out of air. Running out of time. He was trapped somewhere inside one of his town's two elementary schools.

The last radio call stated all the students were out, but a pet rabbit had been left behind. He had been at that section of the school and arrogant enough to believe he could find the rabbit. Instead, he had lost the hand-line. With the oxygen ticking down and the smoke blocking his sight, he needed to find a door or window. He also didn't want his guys to bust his ass for freaking out when someone could be standing ten feet from him. As the captain of the company he needed to remain calm.

His hand slid over a door frame. He searched for the knob and pulled. Two steps in he collided with shelves. Not a way out. A closet. His heart continued to hammer away at his chest, and his lungs fought the short bursts of air he tried to swallow. Panic set in like a bad storm off the ocean, but he couldn't afford the use of energy. He willed his heart to slow and for ice water to run through his veins. The oxygen wasn't gone. Yet. But the tank kept sounding the alarm.

"Phoenix, where are you?" Hawk's voice crackled through the radio.

He just needed three more minutes, and he'd be fine. The door or window was around here somewhere. Hawk would have to wait for a response.

"Captain Egan, please state your location immediately." Hawk's words came through as if his jaw was clenched. His younger brother was trying to remain professional on the radio line and not doing a good job of it.

If he ran out of oxygen, he'd be a dead man. The room filled with increasing heat from the fire that had started in the cafeteria. Once the tank emptied, the instinct was to pull it off for air. If he did that, he'd only manage to burn his lungs instantly. Yeah, he was pretty much fucked in about two minutes.

"Damn it, Phoenix. Where are you? I'm coming."

"I'll figure it out." Somehow. He should be shouting

mayday, but he didn't want Hawk coming for him. Anyone but Hawk.

Stupid. Of course, Hawk would respond first. He carried the guilt of losing Wyatt like a fifth limb. If anything happened to Hawk because he had to come rescue his sorry ass, it would be Phoenix's fault. He couldn't let that happen. Hawk finally had his life together.

"Like hell you will figure it out by yourself." Hawk's words were labored. He was probably trying to run back into the building and through all the smoke. So much for wanting to keep his brother safe.

Phoenix needed to find the damn classroom door. The hose line was right outside it. He dropped to his knees in hopes of gaining some visibility. He bumped into a desk.

Glass shattered in the distance. A crash and bang shook the room. The roof collapsed right behind him. He froze.

"Captain Egan, can you respond?" Chief Wylie's voice jolted him out of his space.

The door was around here somewhere. "I'm fine, Chief."

"Bullshit." Hawk again.

Voices called out over the radio. His crew scrambled, trying to save him. His head hurt. The beeping on his tank picked up speed right along with his heart. Where the fuck was the door?

He crawled across the floor, pushing desks and chairs out of his way. The visibility was maybe four inches. He could be crawling right back to that closet and not know it.

The radio hissed and cracked. The chief called Hawk back to the front of the building. Phoenix hoped his brother followed the order.

His lungs searched for more air. He took a small sip, trying to conserve whatever was left. His head spun. His hand collided with…the rabbit cage. The rabbit jumped in circles in the little space. The teacher had said the cage was by the door.

"You may have saved both our asses." Phoenix shoved the cage under his arm and continued the search for escape.

He followed the change in the floor pattern. He had maybe a minute before he would want to rip his mask off. The oxygen tank's alarm rattled his brain. He stayed on his knees and struggled to find the hose and his way out.

He waited for his lungs to burn. Instead, his hand gripped salvation. *The hose*. He nearly sobbed. With the rabbit under his arm, he hurried along the line.

He slammed into a solid mass. The tank emptied.

"Asshole." Hawk's rough hands dug into his arms.

A sarcastic response tripped across his brain. He wasn't sure if he said it. He might be dead.

ABOUT THE AUTHOR

From an early age, Stacey Wilk told tales as a way to escape. At six she wrote short stories in composition notebooks, at twelve she wrote a novel on a typewriter, in high school biology she wrote rock star romances in her binder instead of paying attention.

But it wasn't until many years later, inspired by her children and a looming birthday, that she finally took her story-telling seriously. And published her first novel in 2013. Since then, she's gone on to publish fifteen more so women everywhere could fall in love and find an escape of their own.

She isn't done telling stories. Not by a long shot. If you want to read her emotional and honest books about family, romance, and second chances, visit her at www. staceywilk.com

To see what she writes next, follow her Facebook group for her amazing readers – Stacey's Novel Family https:// bit.ly/2FK8Lae

Or join her newsletter - https://bit.ly/2A0jEFk

BOOKS BY STACEY WILK

Winter at the Shore Series

No More Darkness

Through the Darkness

Light Upon the Darkness

The Brotherhood Protectors World

Winter's Last Chance

The Last Betrayal

Her Last Word

The Last Days of Christmas

Seduced by Denial

Fighting for Tessa

Nash's Promise

Cruz's Watch (coming Feb. 2024)

The Heritage River Series

A Second Chance House

The Bridge Home

The Essence of Whiskey and Tea

The Big Sky Country Series

Time Won't Erase

Stay Awhile

Love Never Ends (coming 2024)

The Hometown Series - Candlewood Falls world

Taking Root

Raising Winter

Defining Chances

Beginning Over

Steeling Hearts

Whispering Christmas

The Gabriel Hunter Series

Welcome to Kata-Tartaroo

Welcome to Bibliotheca

Welcome to Skull Mountain